Always Wright

Michaela Orme

Moving to Spain, to live with her mother, seemed like the perfect solution to end Sally Wright's problem relationship with her ex – and it might have worked, until she found a dead body.

Suddenly, she is embroiled in a murder investigation and the killer is now chasing her mother.

"A book by a new author ... always a delight to discover, and for most authors always the most difficult to write. 'Always Wright' by Michaela Orme starts on a firm footing and launches the reader straight into the action in Chapter One. Michaela obviously has lived in Spain at some time during her life for she understands the need for her character to abandon attempts at speaking Spanish and resort to speaking English when the pressure is on. I love to write and read stories set in Spain, so I enjoyed this book and very much look forward to reading Michaela's next book."

Hilary Coombes
(author of 'Hen Party' and other novels)
www.hilarycoombes.com

First published in Great Britain in 2019 by U P Publications
Registered Office: St George's House, 14 George Street, Huntingdon, Cambridgeshire, England, PE29 3GH

Cover design copyright © Gaile Griffin Peers 2020

Copyright © Gaile Griffin Peers as Michaela Orme 2019

Michaela Orme has asserted her moral rights

Paperback ISBN: 978-1-912777-06-8
eBook ISBN: 978-1-912777-07-5

9 1 8 2 3 7 6 5 4 0

Published by U P Publications
www.uppbooks.com
www.orme.buzz

Always Wright

Michaela Orme

Dedicated to Mai Griffin and Maisie Orme
for giving unlimited and unfailing support,
so generously

U P Publications
2020

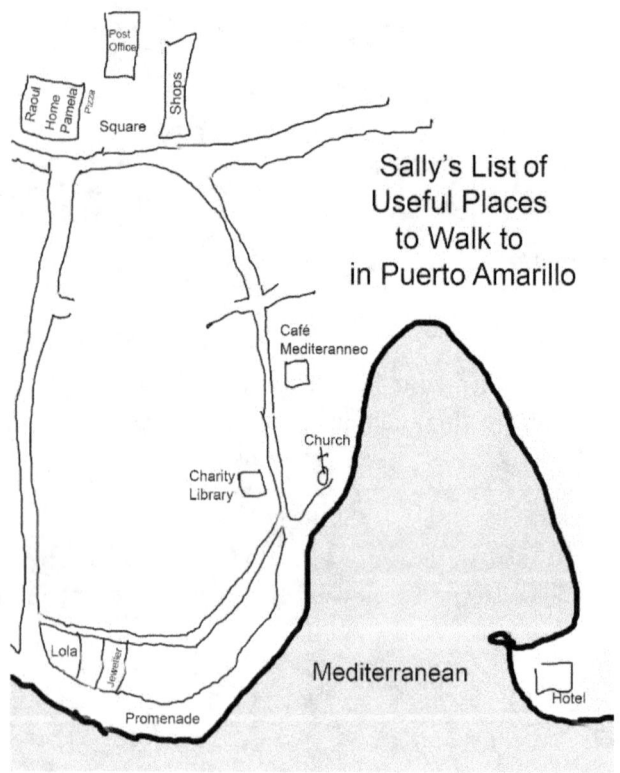

Post Office

Raoul
Home
Pamela
Pizza

Square

Shops

Sally's List of
Useful Places
to Walk to
in Puerto Amarillo

Café
Mediteranneo

Church

Charity
Library

Lola

Jeweller

Mediterranean

Hotel

Promenade

Chapter 1 – Monday Noon

The midday bell from the Fishermen's Church roused Sally from deep contemplation of her coffee cup. How could it possibly be that late? She'd only popped out for a quick breather. A six o'clock start, getting a room ready for her gran's visit, had not been on her agenda until the unexpected call, last night.

Granny Em was due in about seven hours, unless her flight from Cardiff was delayed or the friends she was meeting on the way from the airport, cancelled. Sally was in two minds about whether she was really looking forward to Gran's visit. Her father's mother was never shy about expressing an opinion, and Sally hadn't seen her since breaking up with her fiancé and coming to live with her mother.

Blinking, she took in the bustle along the Mediterranean seafront. Tourists, scurrying to find a table for coffee or wine or lunch, mingled with the locals hurrying to get their chores out of the way before the sun's intensity interfered. Lola was busy with a German customer and Sally listened with admiration as the café-owner effortlessly switched languages from her native Spanish to crisp German. It was no good, languages weren't Sally's forte. She'd tried, notching up three excellent Spanish teachers whose hearts she'd broken with her inability to study and remember the simplest of verbs.

She felt bad for letting them down, but it was probably not surprising. She rarely went anywhere where Spanish was essential and didn't remember to practice it at home with her mother. All Sally knew was that she could manage to make herself understood in most places; the people in her town were the kindest, who, seeing her try, would relent and speak English to her when it was needed.

It was going to be fun going around everywhere with Gran. She probably still had more friends here than Sally and her mother, having lived in Spain for fifteen years. She'd left after Gramps died, to spend time with her younger daughter in England.

When Sally left University, she'd moved nearer her aunt and gran, to carry on her career, so they had both met Sally's ex, which was more than her mother had. She just knew how the conversations would go, once Gran started to tell her mother about him! They might only be in-laws, but she had a feeling that her father's mother and her own would gang up together over this. *Eurgh!* Especially as Gran and Aunt Helen had fallen out over Greg. Her aunt was still completely convinced that Sally had lost a rare gem... *Double Eurgh!!*

Lola finished with the German and was turning towards the next customer, when there was a noisy explosion of plates, cups and glasses, behind her.

"*¡Lo siento, lo siento, lo siento!*" shouted the very upset teenager, who'd just annihilated a table next to the walkway with his out-of-control bike. Sally had often seen fifteen-year-old José weaving in and out of the crowds in the pedestrian area, as he biked up and down the beach-front running errands for his

6

sister, but today was the first time she'd ever seen him fall.

Lola looked furious and didn't seem to care how many *'sorries'* he yelled as she wavered between looking after the shocked people at the adjacent table or rounding on her brother. The upset couple won.

"It was that man with the dog!" the woman at the table nearest to Sally said to her companion. "He was running out of the jeweller's, next door but one, the dog was jumping round him all excited, then it threw itself at the cyclist at the last second. That poor boy was just swerving to avoid the dog and got his bike handle tangled in the tablecloth."

Sally looked behind her, down the sea front, but the culprit had gone by the time she turned. She knew where the jewellery shop was, she could see the stone bench just outside, but it was empty. The area in front of the jeweller's was silent and there were no dogs, jumping or otherwise.

"Where did he go?" she asked.

The women just shrugged and waved vaguely down the promenade.

As Sally got up to leave, Lola was still apologising to guests at the tables near the one that José had wrecked. This wasn't going to be a day for Lola to join her for a glass of wine and a quiet chat. It was too near the lunchtime rush for Lola to take a break, anyway, she noted wryly.

It was also not a day when José seemed eager to chat with his sister either as, yelling more apologies over his shoulders, he grabbed his bike, tried, unsuccessfully, to dislodge the tablecloth, and dashed off back in the direction of the church. Sally thought that his receding comments, delivered in Spanish into the breeze as he pedalled away, was that he'd delivered Lola's message as requested.

Popping the money for the coffee on the table, Sally gave Lola a sympathetic wave and started to head back to her apartment taking the long route, past the jeweller's towards the church, so that she could enjoy the view a little longer and keep an eye open for Lola's tablecloth on the way.

As she walked past the shuttered jewellery shop, she was surprised to see that the door was open. She'd been in the shop a few times and met the owner, Egnacio, which added to her curiosity. He didn't seem the sort to frighten a customer away, once he'd got them in his shop, and he never left his door open, ever. He liked to keep it locked, even when he was open for business. There was a little bell-push so that customers could attract his attention, if they wanted to enter.

Once, when Sally was picking out a gift for her niece's birthday, he'd confided that, for two pins, he would be happier to lock the door when customers were inside too, but he didn't think the Guardia would approve and it might make customers a little nervous – as in 'it is free to come in but you need to buy something before I let you out'. Well, he hadn't locked her in, but he had shut the door. He always made sure his door was shut, even in the hottest weather.

No, he would never leave the door ajar.

Frowning, she walked over to the entrance; there were drops of what looked like red wine on the step leading into the dark little shop, except maybe it wasn't red wine… It was a bit thicker than wine.

Slowly she edged past the drops, for some reason reluctant to step on them. Peering into the dark shop she called out, "Egnacio? Are you there? Why is your door open?"

As Sally stepped nearer to the display counter her eyes began to adjust to the shop's gloom, almost black after the bright sunshine outside. It still took a few seconds before she realised that she wasn't alone.

There was someone sitting in the wooden chair that faced the counter display, but they weren't moving.

"¿Egnacio, que tal?"

Silence.

"Egnacio, are you alright?" Moving forward toward the counter, she discovered the answer.

Glinting in the dim light from the half-open door behind her, the knife protruding from his chest was a pretty big clue that Egnacio wasn't alright and that he would never be able to tell her.

Choking back a scream of horror, she backed carefully out of the shop, making sure not to disturb the drops of what she now knew must be blood. She flopped onto the bench, just outside the shop window and, with shaking hands, grabbed her phone and dialled the police.

As she waited, despite the heat, she felt nauseous and shivery. She closed her eyes for a few minutes and let the warmth of the sun envelop her. After a moment she felt calmer.

When she opened her eyes again, she realised that she was still holding her phone, so she rang her mother to let her know that she would be late home.

It wasn't long before the police arrived. They were quite polite, until they saw the inside of the shop and its dead owner, then they got progressively more aggressive as they shouted questions at her. The faster they spoke, the harder it was for Sally to follow their Spanish. The less she understood, the slower her answers. The slower her answers, the angrier they became. In desperation, she resorted to speaking in English, they were not happy.

Chapter 2 – Monday Afternoon

Sally was bemused. From the moment the police had locked down the scene and started to bombard her with questions in Spanish, she'd been out of her depth.

The more confused she looked, the more they shouted. It was almost funny, as the more they shouted, the more excited they became.

Surely, they knew it was nothing to do with her.

This chaos was not what she'd expected, when watching the quiet street, waiting for the police to arrive. She felt remote, uninvolved. It was as if it were happening to someone else and she was a spectator, looking at the scene from the outside.

The noisier it got, the more detached she felt from what was going on. Her efforts to explain her involvement, in slowly spoken English, had been no more successful than her attempts in 'Spanglish'.

Pedro was surprised as he walked up to Egnacio's jewellery store, where he'd been called to take a statement from yet another foreign resident who spoke no Spanish. No one had bothered to tell him what the crime was or whether she was a witness, victim or suspect. However, given that she obviously spoke little or no Spanish, it could be that the police didn't yet know which she was either.

Sally could feel herself becoming aware of quite unimportant details in the frenzied activity around her. There was hair coming out of the right nostril of the short man waving his hands in her face. The moist forehead of the hatless man trying to keep back curious spectators was not only shiny, it was dripping sweat onto the pavement. The officer with a touch of B.O. was the noisiest interrogator, gesticulating wildly with every phrase. She caught the whiff of his armpits each time he waved his arm.

Pedro decided that she didn't look like a typical victim or incoherent witness. The young woman was stunning: green eyes, brown hair, tall, with an intelligent expression that belied her apparent lack of comprehension about what she was being asked.

To Sally's amusement, the tall man, newest on the scene with a uniform in a different colour from the others, visibly screwed up his nose every time Mr B.O. waved at him.

Officer Tall was well worth concentrating on.

Even a bemused Sally recognised that he was quite the most attractive-looking man she'd seen in a long while: muscular and very easy to look at.

She shook herself – as if she needed to feel any hotter or more bothered, right now, than she already was!

Then she realised that Mr B.O was gesturing the newcomer, to join them. This was not a good way or under the right circumstances to meet someone interesting.

She swallowed and felt dizzy again – standing up had been a mistake; her head was spinning with visions of Egnacio and the knife.

It was a relief when she finally heard a voice speaking English.

"Hi, could I take your name please, mine is Pedro Marcos, I'm with the local police and am here to help you with translation."

It took her a few seconds to focus on an answer.

A sparrow hopped on the bench she'd left when the Guardia had arrived. It cocked its head to one side, focusing on her face, as if it was interested in her answer. "Sally, Sally Wright." she told the bird.

With that, the crowd of policemen around her faded away, melting back into the tableau to resume their various tasks. Even the observers, outside the police tape, seemed more interested in the activity going on inside the shop than in her.

The forensic team, silent from the start, simply carried on with their quiet, meticulous forensic examination of the body and premises.

The Guardia had clearly decided that she was either stupid or knew nothing, so seemed happy to abandon her to the bird and the interpreter who took her arm gently, turning her away from the crime scene to guide her back to the café.

It was only a few steps, but it was enough to help her recover. Once seated again, she surreptitiously studied him, as he ordered a warm drink for her and cold water for himself.

Pedro was tall for a Spaniard, well over the country's average height of five-foot-seven.

At just under six foot, he towered above his diminutive *abuelita* who, at 80, barely topped five-foot-three. Amazingly, she'd managed to raise three sons and a grandson, all at least seven inches taller.

This young woman, however, was only a few inches shorter than he was and while she sipped from a glass of sweet, hot chocolate, for the shock – he realised that her clear, green eyes were level with his.

She looked calm enough to talk, so he got out his phone, set it to record and started the interview, explaining, as he did so, that the recording was to make sure that whatever she said was accurately documented, should she be called as a witness later, or should her statement need to be translated into Spanish.

Sally was grateful that he'd elected to place her so that her view was of the sea, the rocks and the gulls, rather than the forensic team and the chaos a few doors behind her.

She had already looked back once, in the brief time it had taken them to walk to the café. The bench where she'd waited for the police had been vacated by the bird and transformed into a makeshift table. It was already covered in small evidence bags.

It was a relief to be able to turn away and not see it anymore.

Pedro was a nice name, solid, Spanish, trustworthy, and he was tall and handsome with a light-gold Mediterranean tan and intense, but gentle, hazel eyes. However, she needed to get back to her mother and Pedro looked old enough to have a cute wife and a parcel of small children. So, as this was definitely not the time to worry about his marital status, she decided it would be best just to tell him everything she knew, as fast as she could.

Before she started though, she looked towards the table where the two women who saw José's accident had been. They'd gone, but she decided that she'd best start the story with their observations, as there was no doubt in her mind that Egnacio had been murdered by the man whose dog caused the boy's accident, as it ran out of the jewellers.

Carefully recounting all that had happened, from the 'accident' to her curiosity about the open door, she tried to remember if she'd seen anything else.

When Lola came up to their table to see if they wanted anything, Sally realised that Lola, clearing the tables, dealing with the upset clients and fuming over her clumsy brother must have missed what happened. However, she asked if Lola knew the two women.

"I'm sorry Sally, I don't know them. They've been in only once before, the same time, last week. Maybe they'll be here again same time next week, maybe they won't. I can see if they paid in cash or by card, though, if that helps?"

Interested, Pedro asked Lola, in rapid Valencian, for anything she could remember about them, but was disappointed when Lola made a point of replying in English, so that Sally could follow the conversation. "No Señor Marcos, I have no idea about them. If they didn't pay by card, I cannot help you... except that they followed in the direction of my brother José, towards the church. Why don't you see if they are still there, they are tourists and tourists linger in one place for a long while". Ruefully, Lola gestured around her at the tables where several occupants nursed single cups of coffee with no obvious intention of ordering lunch.

Chapter 3 – Still Monday Afternoon

By the time Pedro and Sally had walked along the sea front to the Church, it was a good two hours since the women had left the café. However, there were a lot of tempting restaurants serving lunch on their route, so there was a slim chance that the women were still out and about somewhere nearby. Under normal circumstances, Pedro wouldn't have brought Sally with him, but no more time was to be wasted and she would be able to recognise the witnesses.

Pedro's blue Policía Local uniform drew little attention as he walked beside her. He was a familiar face, unlike the Guardia, in green, who were at the scene of the crime.

He had to be careful, as this was clearly a Guardia case, they handled all serious crimes in towns and villages with populations less than 20,000, like Puerto Amarillo. They also worked with the Policia Nacional who covered crime in larger towns and nationally.

As a local bobby, he had been brought in to liaise, translate and take notes, it wasn't his place to evaluate and solve a murder case.

On the other hand, he really wanted to prolong his meeting with Sally, she was fascinating. His excuse could be that the two women sounded as if they were also British, so might also need an interpreter to collect their information.

He was now glad that his Inspector had moved him from Neighbourhood Patrol to Citizen Security. He wouldn't otherwise have been assigned to the Guardia Civil this morning. Lost in his thoughts and trying to keep up with the pretty young woman striding beside him towards the Church, he almost tripped over when she suddenly stopped.

Sensing that Pedro was distracted by something and wasn't really checking out the streets for the two women, Sally made sure that she looked in as many directions as she could, without going dizzy. They had arrived at the church and she was about to give up when she thought she saw one of the women walking away from a small restaurant, up the hill, ahead of them.

She seemed to be carrying a heavy bag. If she had been to the Charity Bookshop, next to the church, that might explain why she was still in the area. It was the one shop where Sally could easily lose herself for an hour – there were few other places in the port with so many books in English.

Excited to have seen their witness, she turned to Pedro, "One of the ladies is going up the hill next to the church. There! Look!" Turning back and pointing excitedly, she realised that the woman had gone.

How could she have moved so fast with such a big bag?

They ran up the street to the spot where Sally had last seen her, it was a small junction with two narrow streets that criss-crossed the road they'd taken from the church, creating six possible exits.

A myriad of closed and shuttered doorways lining

each of the streets, stared back at them as they checked each in turn, but all were silent. The streets were empty. In the centre of the crossroads was a bag, lying on its side, as if hurriedly dropped. It was emblazoned with the charity shop logo and, spilling from inside, was a selection of second-hand books, in Spanish, English, German, French and Valenciano.

"Maybe the bag got too heavy for her?" Pedro hazarded, "but at least we can ask in the charity shop. Maybe they'll know who she is. If she only spoke in English when you heard her, I wonder why she bought books in so many languages."

"But the shop shuts at two, it will be closed now." Sally felt quite deflated. "And it doesn't open in the evenings, they are all volunteers – tomorrow, it might not even be the same person on duty. Still, José must have seen the man who made him crash, maybe he would be easier to find. He sings in one of the choral groups who do the hymns for the blessings at fiestas, I think that may have been why he was heading up to the church, for practice, perhaps he's still around."

They walked back to the Church, past the emptying Café Mediterraneo, clearing up from its lunchtime rush and passing the shuttered Charity shop.

The Church was not only empty and locked, by the time they arrived, but there wasn't even one member of the choir loitering around the church gate smoking an illicit post-choral cigarette ...a very unusual event!

"Oh well, that's it then." Sally was disappointed. Pedro nodded and looked sad, his excuses for staying with Sally were dwindling, rapidly. "The *Guardia*

Sargento Primero will do the interviews, don't worry, she will trace the women and talk to the boy, I'm just liaison." He fished about in his pockets for a few minutes and pulled out a slim card case, which looked new. "Here is my card, if you think of anything that could help, it has my number, *movil* sorry, my mobile phone number. Meanwhile, let me walk you home, I'm sorry to have taken so much of your time already, today, Senorita Wright".

He paused as his lapel radio squawked his name and screeched a string of fast questions in Valenciano.

Politely he gave her the *'please stay a moment'* signal with his hand and gave answers, just as rapidly back. Having updated his inquisitor on the missing witness and that he had secured the book-bag for forensics to help try and identify her, he finished the conversation and turned back to Sally.

She smiled. "You have been very kind, Señor Marcos - and have helped me get over the shock of finding Egnacio, by giving me something useful to do. But you are right, I must get back to my mother, she will be worried, I live near the Post Office, if that isn't too much out of your way?"

As they walked together, more relaxed now that they had no more searching to do, they started to chat about their lives, where they lived and the places they'd visited.

Sally learned that Pedro was widowed, his wife had died in a traffic accident in Valencia on a shopping trip with friends, as she crossed the busy street to get to the railway station. It might have been quick, but knowing that she hadn't suffered didn't lessen the shock. In the five years of grieving, since her death, Pedro had made no long-lasting relationships.

To his surprise, he was pleased to discover that Sally was recovering from a broken engagement and, even better, that she had chosen to do so by moving to Spain for a complete break. She lived with her mother who was recuperating from breast cancer and glad of the help.

Needless to say, he took no pleasure in her being unhappy, or that her mother had gone through the traumas of breast cancer, but the fact that she would be in Puerto Amarillo for the foreseeable future was definitely brightening his day.

As they neared the post office, *she really must remember to call it Correos*, Sally saw her mother, sitting in the sunshine on a bench at the front. She was chatting to Raoul, who occupied the neighbouring apartment. Raoul's boyfriend was a little flighty and Sally's mother Pamela was his go-to agony aunt.

"Really Pamela, it only takes ninety minutes from the airport at the most but now, on every trip home, Carlos takes two hours, sometimes three. I always check the time the plane lands and, as a steward, he has only cabin luggage. He has no reason to hang around the airport; his home is here. The plane always lands a little earlier than the time due, so why is he taking so long to get back?"

Raoul continued miserably. "He isn't using the same taxi company either. Last month he changed to one based in Alicante and he won't tell me the name. He's being so secretive. We've been together for nearly five years and, in less than a month, it's all falling apart. Please Pamela, say that you will speak to him? I must know the truth. Is he breaking up with me?"

Raoul was so impassioned, waving his arms imploringly, and concentrating so hard on convincing Pamela to help him, that he didn't hear Pedro and Sally arrive, behind him.

Pedro coughed, politely, and couldn't stop a grin as Raoul shot six inches up in the air, twirling about to see who was there. "Oh, Pedro Marcos, I thought it was Carlos, you scared me!"

"Sorry Raoul, not this time, but if you want to talk about him, maybe you shouldn't do it so loudly, in public." Raoul hung his head and looked so guilty that Pedro felt really sorry for him. "Tell you what, Raoul, I have a friend who works at the airport, would you like me to ask him to see what he can find out, quietly?"

"Oooh, Pedro, could you? Please …thank you. He mustn't find out, though, but I need to know. I have to know."

Whilst things calmed down and introductions had been made where needed, Pamela watched her daughter interacting with Pedro and Raoul, who were now teasing each other about some fiesta where Raoul had lost Carlos in the crowd and had been forced to enlist Pedro to find him. Pedro asking everyone at a Moors and Christian parade, if they had seen a pirate, had just been too funny for words. Especially as Raoul had found Carlos, seconds later, but neither of them could now spot Pedro to tell him, so both pirates were forced to walk round the same route asking everyone if they had seen a policeman! It was the first spontaneous laughter she'd heard from Sally since she'd arrived in Spain after she and Greg had split up. It warmed her heart seeing her daughter so carefree.

"So, Sally, how did you and Officer Marcos meet?" she asked, idly. Then wished that she had just stayed quietly listening to them, as her daughter's smile dropped.

Sally's face fell, then clouded even more, when Pedro used the question as an excuse to leave. He needed to return to the seafront to update his Guardia colleagues with all he had learned from her. After Pedro had gone, Sally told her captivated audience about her day, the murder and the chase looking for the women. Even Raoul was distracted by the problem, fanning himself with his newspaper, as he listened.

By the time Pamela and Sally had diverted Raoul enough for him to be able to face his own apartment, they were both tired and decided it was going to be an afternoon with minimal work and an evening of mindless Satellite TV quizzes from the UK, followed by a light supper and an early night, once Granny Em had arrived and settled in.

The snag they discovered, when the doorbell rang at quarter past seven, was that Granny Em had other ideas. It always surprised Pamela, quite how feisty her mother-in-law was. Her eighty years hung relatively lightly on her mind but had taken a toll on her hips and legs.

She *could* walk with a stick but took ruthless advantage of assisted travel and free wheelchair at airports.

"I am eighty, for goodness sake, and I would like to get to a hundred. I'm not going to do that if I don't take every edge I can get! Anyway, to be honest, without my lovely taxi-driver it would have been difficult struggling with my luggage. By the way, he even brought my bags up here for me. Sally can you pay him, dearie, and give him a nice big tip. Then bring the cases in while Pamela makes coffee, I'm parched." Granny Em strode into the sitting room waving her stick around as she went. "Oh, I like what you've done with the place, it looks much better than when I came last year!"

Sally took a deep breath, grabbed her purse and virtually emptied it to pay the taxi-driver's ransom fee. She felt a little like saying, *no we aren't paying it, take her back*. But she couldn't, she really was quite fond of her gran, even if she was totally overbearing.

It was gone midnight by the time they persuaded Granny Em to go to bed. Having brought her up to date with their news and listened to the exploits of Sally's various cousins, they bribed her with the promise of hot chocolate and a nice breakfast in the morning.

Chapter 4 – Sally's Tuesday Morning

Tuesday morning was busy for Sally, she had articles to edit, for *5Ws Magazine,* a UK internet magazine that she still worked for as a proof editor. She was so lucky that her bosses didn't care where she lived, so long as there was internet access. She also had information to gather for her blog page 'Always Wright', on Orme.buzz if she wanted to pick up new clients in Spain.

By the time she'd sorted breakfast out for her mother and gran and submitted the last paragraphs for the magazine, it was half-past-eleven and she realised that, if she didn't move swiftly, the Charity shop would be closed by the time she got there.

Of course, she wasn't being nosey, nor was she going in the hope of seeing Pedro again, she was too busy. No, she was going because she had some books to donate and she was short of something to read, even though, yesterday, she would have said that her mother had so many books she hadn't read yet, that she didn't need to bring home any more.

Instead of going to Lola's café first, tempted though she was to see if José was there, she walked along the road that led straight to the Church.

There was no one in the shop when she arrived except Louise and Harry. They were pleased to have her contribution and, having heard about the murder, were agog to hear, first-hand, how she'd discovered the body.

Louise and Harry were married, having found each other, in their early seventies, through their voluntary work in the Charity Book Shop. Both had children and grandchildren by previous marriages. Louise's last husband was still living in the port and, once Sally had updated them with her news, skating briefly over the drama, Louise lost no time in bringing Sally up to date with hers.

"Fred and his Floozie are going off to Tenerife on holiday. She has put on so much weight since she hooked him, she would look pregnant if she wasn't sixty-three! Far too young for the old goat, even if she looks much older than she is!" She looked at Harry's face, who looked slightly crestfallen at the thought that she might still care and quickly added, "but then, she only has Fred, she doesn't have a really wonderful man in her life to keep looking young for." Louise grinned at Harry and pirouetted gracefully around the bookshelves, not looking anything like her seventy-six years.

Smiling fondly, Harry turned to Sally and asked what author she wanted to explore today. "We have a new book section for local authors – these are only for lending though – as the authors themselves have donated the books. There are some very dark short stories by Vonnie Giles and an interesting World War One Naval story from William Daysh, they live farther up the coast towards Valencia and we have some more coming later in the week – including a paranormal mystery novel."

"That sounds like a great idea, Harry, I'll bring mother in, she might know a few more authors to add to your list. I hope that you are making a small charge to borrow the books?"

"Oh yes, we are asking for a ten-euro deposit, which we refund when the book is returned, less a euro for borrowing it. Nothing too complicated though, else we won't have time to manage it, but it's bringing in people who haven't been here before."

Sally then remembered that she was there to help find the missing witnesses, so she asked if either of them had been on duty the day before.

"Yes, Louise was here with her friend Alice, they never stop talking, so I try and leave them to work together and make myself scarce when Alice is about!"

Louise popped up, at that point. "You cheeky old devil! You know perfectly well, you leave us alone, so you can go have a beer with your old army friends!" She then turned to Sally and questioned why she had asked.

Sally answered with her own question. "Did a middle-aged woman come in after mid-day and buy several books in different languages? Have the police already been in to ask you?"

"Yes, Pedro popped in, first thing this morning with the Guardia Civil Sergeant, a pretty young thing, they asked about the woman who bought a heap of books from the remainders' bin. I told them that she was in here for over an hour and spent more time looking out of the window than at the bookshelves. Then, just before we closed, she grabbed what almost looked like a random pile of books from the bin and piled them on the desk. I think that the carrier bag cost more than the books. I'm surprised that neither of you saw her, you walked past just after she left. Just after two o'clock, she said she had to meet a friend, and rushed off. Then a few minutes later, when I was locking up, I saw you both and wondered if you were expecting to meet her. When she went up the hill so fast, I realised I was wrong".

Barely pausing for breath Louise added, "Why are you interested in her, Pedro wouldn't say. Was it something to do with Egnacio's murder? What did she do? Was she hiding from the police? Was that why she was in here? She's never been in before, as far as I know."

"No, no, no, Louise, nothing like that. I think she saw the murderer, running out of Egnacio's, so Pedro is looking for her, to get a description. I was with him because I saw the woman in Lola's and can identify her. Do you know Pedro, then? I only met him yesterday."

Harry chipped in. "Yes, we both know Pedro, really kind chap. He used to patrol this area, all round the Church and the Beach Restaurants, always made an effort to pop in, every morning, to check we were okay."

Sally felt her cheeks go slightly red, remembering how she'd told Pedro about the charity shop staff and its hours. Oblivious, Harry continued. "We were quite sad when he got his new job in Citizen Security, though Roberto, his replacement, seems quite pleasant. But we are just being selfish, it's a great thing for Pedro, it means he'll work on more interesting cases. He seemed quite excited about working with the pretty First Sergeant, too, though that might be because he gets to liaise with the Guardia Civil now, when the Inspector lets him, even if it is only legwork!"

Seeing the strange, uncertain look that flitted across Sally's face, Louise added, gently "I think that they were heading down to Lola's, next, if you want to catch him." Sally shrugged to hide her embarrassment, picked up a Rankin book that she hadn't read yet and, after paying for it, left the shop heading firmly away from Lola's Café. It was time she got back to the apartment anyway. Goodness only knew what matchmaking plans Pamela and Granny Em would make, if she left them alone for too long.

Chapter 5 – Pamela's Tuesday Morning

As soon as Granny Em surfaced, she headed straight out to sit in the cool of the restaurant, where Pamela could hear the chatter through the open window. Her mother-in-law sounded very happy as she held court with a series of old friends, as each came in to buy her coffee and say hello. When she looked out of the window, to check up on her, Emma was waving a camera around and taking random photos of the square and her visitors then showing the pictures to her victims.

Emma wasn't ever quiet for long. It had taken some getting used to, when Pamela first started going out with Emma's son. Emma had simply absorbed Pamela into the family and treated her like a daughter from day one. It was nice that, whenever Emma visited, she never made a fuss. She'd always treated Mark and Pamela's home like her own. It did grate a little, though, when Pamela wanted privacy or to make plans, but it was also a huge comfort when Mark died. Even though she'd lost her son, Emma always made it clear that Pamela's grief and dreadful loss were on a par with her own and she'd made time, in that black period, to be there for Pamela and ensuring that Sally was OK.

On this trip however, the more time Emma spent

wandering about and visiting, the less she would be underfoot, and the more time Pamela would have for herself and Sally.

Satisfied that Emma was happily occupied, Pamela decided to spend the morning working on the dress details of a portrait.

She didn't need her sitter for the minutiae of the painting. She'd seated a mannequin on the chair the sitter had used and had draped the dress to match the photos she'd taken when she and the sitter had first agreed the pose. It was a beautiful creamy-yellow dress, with a lot of embroidery and lace around the traditional Spanish bodice. This was the costume being worn by *la Reina de les Fogueres*, the Queen of the Bonfires.

Every year, the port celebrated mid-summer with a fiesta that included bonfires, fireworks, processions, children and adults. Pretty much everyone in the port was involved in the event. It was also the annual event when Puerto Amarillo traditionally recognised the coming of age of its youth, with each of the main streets in the town putting forward their daughters and sons (who had turned eighteen since the last fiesta) for blessing and recognition. An honoured few of the girls were selected as ladies-in-waiting for the girl elected as the queen, and the boys vied to be the honour guard of whichever of them was elected king.

It was a huge honour for the families chosen, but it involved the whole community, as each of the selected families would have to put entertainments on for their quintas and their streets. The King and Queen's families also made a big contribution to the entertainment of all involved.

The costumes of the ladies in waiting were based on traditional 19th century Spanish court dresses and were made especially for each girl, often costing each of the girls' families more than 2000 euros.

The Queen's costume had to be even more flamboyant than theirs and this one had crystals embroidered into the bodice that flashed in the sunshine. She tried to remember who'd made the dress. It was someone new, a real find, some dressmaker from Madrid who'd just moved into the port somewhere near Lola's Café.

Pamela was very proud to have been selected to paint the portraits of each Festival Queen for the last three years.

It was a huge honour for a foreigner, and she loved doing it, but there was a lot of detail in the clothes. The families commissioning the portraits wanted the expensive dresses to shine almost as much as their daughters, as the portraits would be a lasting memento of their reign and 'importance'.

It was a pleasure to work in her studio, so she was happy to occupy herself painting, until Sally finished working and went out, but it was tiring. Once she was alone, she would take a recipe over to Raoul, as an excuse to stop, rest and chat and find out a little more about all the strange things that Carlos had been doing to upset his partner.

Painting took a lot of concentration and was tiring on her arms. It had been several months since her last operation, the final rebuilds, after her double mastectomy, and even longer since her last chemo, but she still tired quickly.

As much as she was enjoying bringing the intricate details of the dress to life, it was a relief to hear Sally calling out a quick good-bye before leaving.

With an exhausted sigh, Pamela was glad to lay down her brush and start tidying up. Once the brushes were clean, she wrapped her palette in plastic film and popped it onto the 'work in progress' shelf in the studio fridge.

People were often surprised at how little mess she made, when painting, but she had been brought up by a pair of wartime babies and both parents had instilled their austerity upbringing on her. They had hated waste. A clean artist and studio saved time, unnecessary laundry and paint!

She shrugged away her regular worry 'am I really a bit OCD?' and checked herself in the mirror, just in case she had dropped paint on herself.

Nope, she hadn't. She was ready to go.

Going to Raoul was really an excuse to rest, without feeling guilty, while he chatted. Raoul's family owned a small bodega, on the inland edge of the port, so he could always be relied upon to have a good red wine ready to be opened and shared.

Raoul was delighted to have some company and an excuse to open a bottle of wine. Although he'd been brought up completely Spanish, his grandmother was the daughter of a French vineyard owner in Provence, so he always felt that he and his father had an added exotic pedigree in the wine business. A man with an excellent palate, Pamela thought, as she relaxed on his balcony nursing a glass of a superb local *vino tinto* and listened to him chatter about the latest gossip. His windows overlooked the other side of the building from the square. It was quieter on this side and his balcony, sunny in the morning, was shaded in the afternoon. This suited Raoul. Like many of his compatriots, he valued shade more than direct sunlight. He thought it was funny when British residents complained about their right to light and had laws in their country to enforce it, in his country the law supported the right to shade, much more precious in his eyes.

Too much sun could kill you!

"So, Pamela, glad though I am to have the recipe, that was not why you came, you want to know if anything else has happened with Carlos and you want to know all about Pedro, yes?"

Pamela laughed. "Am I so transparent?"

"Pfft, *si*, you are a mother Pamela, and a good friend, so of course you worry about us, that is nice." Raoul refilled her glass and then told her about last night. "Carlos should have been home by nine o'clock, but he didn't get in until half past ten. His paella was almost dry and solid by the time he came in, it had simmered for so long. But maybe he'd eaten as he just looked tired and he didn't eat much. He is not happy, my *hombre*, I am not happy, but maybe it is his work that makes him fret, he says he loves me… I think he loves me… but he isn't talking to me about this missing time."

They chatted and speculated until neither could think of anything more that could explain why Carlos had been late every flight for a whole month.

"Maybe Pedro will find the answer for you... and talking of Pedro?"

"Aah... Pedro." Raoul smiled, wistfully, "my first love!"

Pamela almost choked as her wine went completely the wrong way.

"Is he...?"

"No, sadly he is not, but that didn't stop me having a huge crush on him, when we were at school together! He was a couple of months older than me and a prefect around the time I discovered that girls didn't interest me, like they interested most of the other boys. This is Spain and this isn't something that has always been easy to discuss. Our parents grew up under Franco's restrictive regime. The freedom to speak and do almost as we wish was something new to their generation. So, I never told anyone how I felt."

Raoul sipped his wine, "I don't know if Pedro ever guessed how I felt about him then, but I know he was always kind. When I was bullied for wanting to wear lace and pretty shirts at the summer fiesta, he suggested that our quinta modelled our costumes on our favourite bullfighters – so we all wore costumes nearly as embroidered as the girl's, though Pedro looked quite handsome and macho in his. I was at his wedding six years ago and, barely a year later, I was with him when he got the message about his wife having been hit by a drunk driver. I drove him to Valencia that night and have never, ever, felt so useless. It was so sad, so stupid, so wrong, that a man with a heart as good as his should be so unhappy."

He paused, thoughtfully. "Whereas me? What have

I done? Now I am unhappy, but I still have Carlos, I haven't yet lost him, so I shouldn't be unhappy, I should be happy!"

With a rueful smile Raoul gazed at the now empty bottle and Pamela decided that she'd best get back to see if any of her stray flock had come home.

Chapter 6 – Tuesday Lunch

The last person Sally expected to see as she approached the door of her mother's apartment was Pedro. With him was a petite and very pretty Spanish woman in the green uniform of a Guardia Civil *Sargento Primero*. They stood outside the door, presumably waiting for her mother to answer the bell.

They were talking, animatedly, in what she thought must be Valenciano again, as it didn't sound like the little Spanish she knew. It was strange how many officials here seemed to prefer Valenciano to the National language of Spain, Castilian. All she understood, from their rapid exchange before they noticed her, was her name, Sally, and something about José.

The woman smiled at her and in broken English asked if she was Sally Wright. "I, First Sergeant Sofía Gonzales *de Guardia Civil*, you 'elping me?" Sergeant Gonzales purred softly, in what Sally thought must be a very sexy voice, judging by Pedro's tight smile as he looked at Sally.

He waited, politely, for the sergeant to pause and added, "Señorita, we need to ask you some more questions about yesterday – please may we come in?"

This wasn't how she'd imagined showing Pedro where she lived, in the idle moments before she'd fallen asleep last night. No well-cooked dinner, no candles and too much First Sergeant Sofía Gonzales. She might be little, *sorry,* petite, but she oozed sexiness, even Sally could feel it and she'd never looked at another woman that way.

She let them into the apartment, calling out to her mother that they had guests, as she opened the door.

The flat's entrance led into a long hall. On the left was a big kitchen, a dining room and the guest bedroom that Sally had commandeered as a study, soon after arriving, but which was now strewn with discarded support tights and Granny Em's partially unpacked suitcases. On the right was Pamela's bedroom, her ensuite, the main bathroom, and Sally's bedroom, much smaller than the study opposite, but she spent as little time in there as she could, so sleeping space wasn't as important as having a large office.

The corridor's end spilled into the main living space, a large, airy, triple-aspect room that ran the width of the apartment. Opposite the corridor, on the far side of the room, French doors opened onto a balcony, that overlooked the square. It was as long as the apartment was wide and perfect for romantic evening dinners for two, while creating welcome shade for the outside tables of the small restaurant, underneath.

As Sally led them into the main room, gesturing to the seats, she asked if they would like coffee or a glass of wine, unsure if they were stopping by before or after their lunch break, assuming that the police stopped to eat at lunchtime.

Politely, they both refused. Sergeant Gonzales

seemed impressed with the apartment, but she wasn't from Puerto Amarillo. Pedro seemed to take the space and comfort of the flat for granted, but he would have grown up surrounded by the grand eighteenth-century townhouses that made up the centre of the pueblo. He'd probably known most of them, before they'd been broken up into flats, so for him this was just half of the top floor of the palatial family house this had once been.

Clustered around the north window of the living room, on the right, to catch the North light on her canvas when she was painting, was Pamela's easel and studio area, partially screened from the rest of the room by tall bookshelves that created the illusion of a room inside a room. Pamela had lived on her own for a long while and wasn't a messy painter so, as Sally had lived with the smell of oil paint and turpentine all her life, she had seen no reason to disrupt her mother any more than was necessary. The rest of the room, artificially L-shaped by the studio space, was elegantly furnished with two leather settees, two matching recliners, a large flatscreen TV and several oriental teak and glass cupboards full of exotic ornaments and Chinese antiques, the fruit of Pamela's lifetime of travelling round the world, plying her trade as a portrait painter.

The two police officers sat where she'd indicated and absorbed the décor.

The walls of the wide hallway and the living area (and pretty much every room they could see into) were lined with Pamela's oil paintings – landscapes, still-life and family portraits including one that must have been Sally aged about six, Pedro decided, captivated by the child's eyes that, he was sure, had followed his progress down the hall.

Pedro cleared his throat and, after a nod from the sergeant, explained why they still needed help.

José had seen the dog, a dachshund, as it pelted out of the jewellers, its red leather lead flying. The dog had looked scared. Trying to avoid the dog, panicking about being late for choir practice and needing to avoid being detained by an angry sister, he'd been cycling too fast to react properly and had crashed into the table. José hadn't seen anything else. He was vaguely aware that the man following the dog was waving what looked like a large blue hankie, or maybe a small scarf, but he only saw that because it was something else that was moving on the periphery of his vision, as he fell.

He *thought* the man didn't look Spanish, because his mental reaction to the catastrophe was *damned tourist*, but fat or thin, tall or short, no idea …pale skin was all he could be sure about, untanned, maybe…

"So, your ladies may be the only witnesses with a clear view. We have traced the German couple that Lola was dealing with, but they had their backs to the jeweller's shop and were facing away from the café to enjoy the view of the harbour. When they turned towards the shop front, they were talking to the waitress and, on the few times they looked in that direction, Lola was screening the two women. You too were facing the sea, but from deeper inside the café's terrace, which is why you had such a good view of both the women. They, facing towards you, had an unobstructed view of the jewellery store, beyond your table." Pedro paused, he'd just said something significant, he could see it in Sally's face, she must never play poker, unless it was with him. "Yes, you have remembered something?"

"Well, not remembered, exactly" Sally stumbled, not wanting to sound vague or stupid, especially with that bombshell of a sergeant scrutinising her so closely. "It's just that, people go to Lola's for the amazing views of the sea, the port, the boats – I mean," she stumbled, trying not to sound disloyal to her friend, "I mean that Lola has great food and makes nice coffee, but people do tend to go there for the view. She didn't know either of the women, it was only their second visit. So why?" she asked, "Why were they facing away from the sea? Why were they looking inland, along the sea front, at the people and shops and not at what everyone one else was looking?"

Pedro and Sofía looked at each other. Sofía nodded, he was smart and had been right to bring her to talk to his pretty new friend again, Sally had seen more than she realised, and this information was one of the missing bits of the puzzle that had been gnawing at the edges of her mind. Now, she knew why the image she'd formed had felt wrong.

She smiled at Sally, a real smile, that transformed her face from a professional look of constant suspicion, to one of a warm and potential new friend. "Brilliant Sally, *gracias*, that is it. That was what has been at the back of my head? ...mind, since Pedro gave me your statement ...disappearing witnesses who were looking the wrong way, mmm."

Pamela had still not appeared from wherever she was, when, a few minutes later, Pedro and Sofía made their excuses and left, so Sally had time to collect her thoughts and start writing up a list of what she knew and what she guessed about Egnacio, the witnesses the man, the dog and the murder, before her mother came in.

Over lunch, Sally showed her notes to her mother while she summarised her day. It was a depressingly short list.

Chapter 7 – Tuesday Afternoon

Pedro was pleased that Sally had impressed First Sergeant Gonzales, he hoped that it would give him a chance to spend a little more time with Sally while he was on duty, then maybe a little time when he was off duty.

Thinking about Sally reminded him of the promise he'd made to Raoul. He made a note on his phone to ring his friend who ran the staff cafeteria, behind the duty-free zone in Alicante Airport. He knew a lot of the Spanish aircrew, as they would often pop in, between flights, and chat about the places they were visiting and things that happened on the flights. It was still a longshot that he would even know Carlos, but, if Carlos was spending time at the airport, before coming home, maybe it was in the bar.

He thought about his day; it had been a long one. He still wasn't sure what track Gonzales was on, she definitely had a bee in her bonnet now, about finding the women, even though they might have other leads for the man and the dog.

Because José identified the dog as a dachshund, he and Roberto, after parting from Gonzales, spent the rest of the day going around local vets to get lists of all dachshund owners they had on their books. There weren't as many dachs owners as he'd expected, in fact, so far, they'd only found five. Even better, three of the dachshunds were black and tan brindled wire-haired but the dog that José described was smooth and black. Tomorrow, he and Gonzales would visit the remaining two dog owners on their list, while Roberto would check the last, more distant, vet in the area, just in case.

The list wasn't foolproof. The man with the dog might not be its owner, he might have no connection with the Port and been visiting from another town along the coast. But, maybe, just maybe, they would be lucky. Mañana was looking hopeful.

Harry and Louise had a good morning in the shop, with several gifts from tourists who wanted to donate their completed holiday reading material, rather than fill their return luggage with books they'd now read. Of course, many visitors used tablets and e-readers and didn't want to cart around actual books, but there were still enough people who appreciated holding a real book, to keep the charity shop going. It was hardly a good idea bringing a tablet to the beach where you couldn't leave it while swimming and, unlike a book, it was risky taking one onto a lilo in the pool.

Louise had just started reading one of the 'books by local authors' called "Ghostly Echoes" and was so completely absorbed, that when Harry put his hand on her shoulder, she jumped a mile. There is nothing more likely to make a person jump than being startled while reading a spooky book!

Harry was waving at the window with his other hand. He'd just seen the woman who'd run away from Sally and Officer Marcos. She was walking up the hill, as she'd done the day before yesterday, only this time she wasn't encumbered by a bag full of books.

Excited, Louise dashed to the window and watched the woman and where she was heading, while Harry rang Pedro.

"Tell Pedro she is just turning down Calle San Sebastian, from the junction where she dropped the books, the other day. No, wait, she has stopped and is coming back down the hill very fast, she is almost running. Ahh, she's gone off the street into Café Mediterraneo. Now a man has just come out of San Sebastian and is turning round and round, like Pedro and Sally did the day before yesterday. Maybe he is looking for... *What does he look like?* Shh Harry, I'm trying to tell you! – Quick, give me your phone... Well STOP talking to Pedro, there's no time dear. Just give me your phone."

With surprising dexterity for a septuagenarian, Louise seized Harry's phone, ended the call, pushed the camera icon and managed to get two distant photos of the man before he stamped off back down Calle San Sebastian. "There!" she said triumphantly. "His picture is on your phone now, so you can send the photos to Pedro, while I grab my bag and my own phone. I am going to see if that woman is still in the Café, if she is, I'll pretend I'm taking a selfie and see if I can get a photo of her too. Once Pedro has the photos, you can close the shop and come and join me, whether she's still there, or not, we have earned a nice lunch, don't you think?"

Before Harry could ask what a 'selfie' was, or protest that she shouldn't be dashing about playing detective with a killer at large, she was halfway up the hill to the café.

Sighing, he looked at his phone and tried to work out how to send the photos. It was no good, Louise was much more technical than he was – she was a real silver surfer, he was more a balding pink beach toy. He gave up and phoned Pedro back, instead.

Pedro said he would head straight for the café and meet them both there in ten minutes.

Luckily, when Harry called, Pedro and Sofía had just finished interviewing the last dog owner on their list. OK, it wasn't a long list but no matter the length, he wondered, why is it always the last one who has information, never the first? ...And worse, the last one was always at the top of a steep hill, or at the end of a mile-long street! Not that he disliked walking, but he also liked his car and his motorbike. "Boy's toys" Raoul called them, plus the last few days had involved more walking for the Guardia than he'd done when on Neighbourhood Patrol and that job was *all* about walking. Maybe it was missing all those chats and coffee whenever he stopped that made a difference.

Still, Harry's call couldn't have been better timed. Frau Schmeckler, the dachshund owner he'd just interviewed with Sergeant Gonzales, had recently employed a dog-walker to exercise her precious Fritz, *"with his custom-made red leather lead"*, as she hadn't been well and the hills in the port were too tiring for her. "Until they open a dog park near the *punto verde* on this side of the town, I have to have someone else to take darling Fwitzy for his wittle walks."

It only took the sergeant's petting the dog a few times before they managed to get the name of her dog-walker – a friend of a friend who was an acquaintance of someone who worked in the Indian Restaurant in the old Harbour and who'd suggested that they had a regular customer who might be glad of some cash. Herbert, she thought his name was, Herbert Loomas, that was it. Yes, he came highly recommended, did they need a dogwalker for their police dog? Sofía and Pedro exchanged glances – she was clearly demented...

It was a relief when Harry's call came, just after they'd extracted Herbert's address and phone number.

After a brief discussion, the sergeant decided that she would let Pedro handle the witness and the staff from the Charity Shop.

If this address panned out, she'd have Herbert in custody by the end of the afternoon and the woman would only be needed to corroborate his guilt, not to find him.

It took Sofía a good thirty minutes to get back to her car, find the address on her GPS and then, having arrived, to find parking.

Apparently, Herbert had a place in one of Puerto Amarillo's few urbanisations. A group of small villas clustered around a community pool, mostly holiday villas from the look of it. There were a lot of cars with hire-company stickers in their back windows. She grimaced; if ever she went abroad and hired a car with a conspicuous label stuck on it, she would peel it straight off. It was like a poster saying *"Hey, I'm being driven by a tourist who has probably left a nice camera, a passport and some cash in me"*.

Herbert was meant to live at number 53. It wasn't a big urbanisation area, so it didn't take long for her to walk up and down the street twice. No, there was no 53. She counted the houses again, under her breath... forty-two. Even with the bizarre numbering system employed by the Town Hall, there was no house numbered fifty-three.

To make doubly sure, the sergeant called at several of the occupied villas and established, beyond certainty that Herbert had never lived in any part of the street.

Sofía was more than a little frustrated. Another dead end.

She made her way back to her car and rang her office, to report in and check on any progress they were making, before she went home.

This was not her day! The coroner wanted her to attend the initial autopsy but would not be available until eight that evening. Capping that, the office was still waiting for the Tourist Office to release all the Port's CCTV footage. The Tourist Office staff were trying to co-operate, but the technician who managed the port's small CCTV installations was on holiday and, as a small pueblo with a low crime rate, this was not something that many of the staff had ever dealt with.

Officially, she was told that the formal request for copies of the Tourist Office's CCTV footage was being processed. Unofficially, her boss advised her to send an IT literate local, round the shops and buildings with security cameras, near the crime scene, rather than rely on the Tourist Office camera. So, next, she rang in and asked if the Policía Local could supply officers to view the footage taken at the various locations. EU rulings allowed for police inspection of security and video footage under the Data Protection Regulations at the premises where they were recorded – providing there was sufficient cause to justify the request, but for the police to get hold of copies and take them away, it required paperwork, more paperwork and after that …a fair amount of paperwork!

She wasn't expecting a lot. It was unlikely that there would be any solid leads from the local shops that actually had security cameras but it *would* be easier to send the officers out to view the video footage in situ rather than wait for the shops to agree to send their footage to her.

The other consolation over the delay was that the first Tourist Office camera's view was of the area in front of the Marina and the beach. Although it looked down the sea front, towards Lola's Café – it was some distance away and the images would not be clear, anyway. Once they had their suspect in custody it would help to secure a conviction, but she doubted that it would be enough to find him.

The second camera was near the Post Office and pointed half into the square and half onto the street that came up from the Church. It was only designed to capture fiesta processions and give an idea of the traffic.

She sighed. Whilst it was a crucial step for her career to be handling this investigation – it was also critical that she succeed and make a convincing arrest. At least she was lucky to be able to co-opt the local police into helping – there were disadvantages in trying to conduct an investigation of this seriousness in a sleepy little port where murders just didn't and shouldn't happen.

Before driving back to the office, she rang Roberto, to let him know that they might have identified their suspect, even if they hadn't managed to find him yet. Cheering her up a little was his news; Roberto had just seen the last vet and now had three more names, if Herbert wasn't their man.

Chapter 8 – Louise's Tuesday Afternoon

By the time Harry had locked up and walked up the hill to the Café, Louise was on her own, at the table near the window she'd selected *"for the best view"*.

She was bubbling with excitement. "The woman, she knows the owner, I only just managed to get a blurry photo of her before she disappeared into the back of the restaurant. I thought, at first, that she'd gone to the bathroom, but she walked straight past it, into the owner's office. I don't know, though, if she is still in there, or if she has gone out through another door."

She paused long enough for Harry to sit and order a *cerveza*. "Why don't we come here more often? They have a pensioner's menu for ten euros, although today's special is *albóndigas* and I don't like meatballs."

They finally settled on Spanish Omelette for Harry and Roast Chicken for Louise and, as it was served quickly, they were nearly finished by the time Pedro joined them.

He sat at their table, but waved the menu away, much to the curiosity of the waitress.

Louise sent her photo of the woman to his phone and, discovering that Harry hadn't managed to send the ones on his phone, sent those as well.

While Pedro looked at the photos, Louise went over her activities, ending with the woman disappearing into the office.

"It is quite odd, how elusive this witness is being, she looked quite frightened when she dashed into the restaurant, so if she was going to run through and go out of the back, why didn't she go straight away, why was she still in the main café, when I arrived, long enough for me to capture her photo? Not that it's particularly well focussed, I don't have much call to use it."

Pedro was also puzzled, it was almost as if the woman was deliberately trying to avoid being questioned, so did she know that Egnacio had been murdered, maybe she'd recognised the man? Or perhaps she knew a lot more about what had happened than anyone imagined? Where was her companion, the other woman? She hadn't been seen at all, by anyone, since they left Lola's Café.

First, he must go through to see if she was still there and to talk to the restaurant's owner to discover what he had to say. He might even have the answers.

Smiling his thanks for the photos, even though he hadn't recognised either subject, he told his friends to enjoy the rest of the meal, on him; he would take care of the bill as a thank you for their help. He thought, as he walked across the restaurant, that, although he didn't make a huge amount as a policeman, he was better off than his English *pensionista* friends, constantly worrying about exchange rates, and it was nice to be able to say thank you in a way they could enjoy.

Always Right

It was unlikely that she would still be in the restaurant, so he saw no point in rushing. After he'd settled their bill with the waitress, he went to the door through which the woman had gone and, knocking first, went in.

Harry and Louise waited a while, after their dessert and coffee, but he didn't reappear and they couldn't wait much longer, their siesta was calling and then there were English soaps to watch on their satellite television, so they put the day's real drama to one side, for a while, and went home to the vicarious thrills of love triangles and unfaithful friends on TV.

Pedro's first surprise, when he went into the office, was that the woman Louise had snapped was still in there. She was sitting at the manager's desk, going through paperwork.

His second, now that he could see her clearly, was when he realised that he'd seen her before a few weeks ago, with a young girl from the Port.

Her name was Marianne Thompson and she'd just moved to the Port, from Alicante, to teach in the English school. Her speciality was Mathematics and, in her spare time she'd worked in the UK as a bookkeeper.

Mario, the restaurant owner had asked for her help to get his papers in order, for his *gestor*, she knew only a little about Spanish accounting, but enough to be able to able to help get the paperwork together ready for the accountant.

She did not look happy to have been found and claimed to have been unaware of the murder. After

53

some persuasion, Pedro eventually managed to get her story - It was her friend who'd seen the accident and had drawn her attention to the fracas. Her friend wasn't English, although she spoke it very well. She was Valentina Karkoff from Madrid. They hadn't known each other long, but she was sure that she had her details in her address book, which was back at her house.

She gave Pedro directions and he arranged for an officer to call in on her later to collect the information. First, however, he phoned the sergeant, as he felt sure that she would want to interview both the women as soon as possible, then he waited for her to arrive and interview Marianne to get more details.

Harry and Louise had long gone, by the time First Sergeant Sofía Gonzales and Pedro left the restaurant. Marianne lived on Roberto's patrol route, so Sofía had arranged for him to pick up the local information about Valentina's address and then she rang her contact in the Policia Nacional to see what information they held on Marianne, Valentina and Herbert.

Sofía felt strongly that something didn't add up.

Witnesses to violent incidents were normally falling over themselves to come forward and tell their stories, to share phone videos and photos. Most were even keen to share their horrific experiences with the press.

It was improbable that neither of the women had heard of the murder. By now, the port and local papers were buzzing with information.

So, even if they had been unaware at the time, of the importance of what they'd seen, they must have realised before today. Marianne, however, had feigned complete ignorance of the murder, to justify why she hadn't come forward.

This was the first time, in Sofía's experience, when everyone who had useful information had totally disappeared; they were two days into this investigation and still trying to track witnesses down. Maybe she was just tired. It would be a while yet before they got the full forensics report from the crime scene.

Forensics were bogged down with an ever-growing backlog from Barcelona incidents, which took priority over everything. Until the results were back, she was working blind. It was certainly not the fault of the local police force; they'd been excellent here. Pedro had got a lot of useful information through his network.

It was tough being a young mother and being a Guardia Civil *Sargento Primero*, but it had been hard work earning her stripes and just as her bosses hadn't wanted to lose her, she hadn't wanted to give up her work.

It had been a long first year after her daughter was born, but she was gradually getting into the rhythm of balancing life, her daughter and work, and her husband was wonderful. His work as a web-developer gave him flexible hours to work round her hours, however mad they got.

Maybe, when this was over, she would enjoy having friends to visit in Puerto Amarillo.

Egnacio's son, however, wouldn't be on her

dinner invitation list.

He was a nasty middle-aged man, with a pinched face and an unpleasant habit of picking at his nose, whilst he was listening to what was being said to him.

She'd expected him to be a little more upset about his father than he appeared to be, but other than wanting to do a stocktake for the estate valuation, as fast as was possible, he'd expressed little emotion over his father's violent end.

She found that strange.

It wasn't criminal, but it was strange.

On the other side of town, Greg looked out, drinking in the warm sunshine that poured onto the balcony. He grabbed a beer from the bedroom's small fridge and stepped into the heat of the day.

Once he'd pushed a chair towards the shade of the umbrella, he sat in it, savouring the warmth and the excellent view that the hotel suite gave him. Quietly sipping from the glass, he gazed down into the lives of all the small souls scurrying up and down the harbour promenade.

Calmly and carefully he scrutinised the promenade, the beach and the walkways, willing Sally to come into view, he was sure she would, she had written quite detailed, gossipy letters to Helen, so he already knew all her favourite haunts.

Sooner or later he would spot her and then the fun and games could begin!

Chapter 9 – Sally's Tuesday Evening

Sally was glad that her mother had only been next door. There was a lot to tell her and she wanted to see how the portrait was going.

Yes, it was silly, she could have looked any time while Pamela was out, but it was part of their ritual; Pamela always liked to be there when Sally looked at her latest progress, so that she could watch Sally's face. After all, as her mother, Pamela had known her face all her life and knew the tell-tale signs of pleasure or dislike that flicked across it, which others might not notice.

Sally wasn't certain about the portrait commission, she'd seen the amount of decoration on the dress and was worried, not that Pamela couldn't paint it; of course she could, she would do a brilliant job. No, she was worried about how tiring it was for her mother to work on it. The concentration and the level of detail meant she would be leaning over the painting with her arms up in the air for long periods. It was a relief to know that she'd been sensible enough to stop this morning, to spend time with Raoul and relax a little.

They walked through to the Studio area after a light and late lunch on the balcony and Pamela was pleased to see Sally's spontaneous smile when she saw the work she'd done that morning.

57

"It is lovely, mother, one of your best yet."

The crystals on the canvas reflected the light with the same sparkle as the dress on the mannequin, perhaps even more so. In the painting they looked real.

"What happens to the dresses when the fiestas are over for the year? I've always wondered," Sally asked.

"Well some families just keep them, I suspect that some may cannibalise the most expensive elements of the dress to make dresses for other family members, as they need them. Others are sold through the seamstress who made them, so that they can be adapted for girls in another town, another year. A few of the ladies-in-waiting will be wearing dresses like that, this year, that are hired, although this one isn't. It is very much bespoke." Pamela paused thinking about a visit she'd made to a business exposition in Alicante a few years ago.

"Do you remember, I told you about a trade fair near Alicante Airport that promoted local port businesses? We all trooped down to support them." Pamela waited for Sally's nod before continuing, "Well, there were a couple of other events going on in the Exhibition Halls at the same time. One was an equestrian event, the other was an exhibition of Fiesta costumes."

She smiled at her memories, it had been a lovely weekend, one of the last with Mark, Sally's father. "It was amazing. There were dressmakers and designers from all over Spain, showing off the most fabulous costumes to buy or rent. They had dresses for every fiesta – Moors and Christians, the *Fogueres*, even the Three Kings after Christmas – everything that anyone involved could ever need. They send the costumes to and from towns all over the world, anywhere that they might have a market. There were stalls from Brazil, Argentina and Peru, it was quite amazing. There were stalls with accessories and sparkly costume jewellery and some stalls had jewellery made of gold set with valuable jewels. I took some photos while I was there. I'll see if I can find them later, you'll love the dresses. Your father nearly bought me a necklace, but he felt unwell, halfway round, so we went back to the hotel early".

Feeling saddened now, they both went back to finishing off their various chores for the day.

Granny Em came back extremely happy from her day of catching up with old friends. So much so, that she was thinking about going off with one of them for a day trip. "I had forgotten how tall and good-looking Miguel is. So sorry to hear about his wife, but she left him very well off. Who would have thought that he hasn't been snapped up yet? He arrived at the café with a glorious bouquet of flowers and my favourite chocolates. I always think it's a good sign when a man remembers my favourite chocolates." She foraged in her handbag and pulled out a small camera from it. "I forgot to show you this, I bought it in Duty Free on the way out here, it is a lovely light little thing and I thought I would have fun taking photos of all my favourite places, while I was here, I have so few from when your Grandad was alive. Look, these are from today…" She passed the camera to Sally who duly admired it and the pictures on it of her gran's old friends, only a few of whom she knew. When she'd finished looking through, she gave the camera to her mother. Pamela asked a question about an old mutual friend, so Em grabbed her glass and sat next to Pamela, to make it easier to chat about the people in the photos as Pamela looked through them. In no time they were deeply involved in reminiscences of parties and events from when Pamela and Em's son Mark had first come to live in Spain.

Escaping from the stream of chatter, knowing that, after a few glasses of wine, the stories would get quite saucy, Sally headed to the kitchen to tackle the huge bouquet of red roses and dramatic pink lilies that had been tossed, unceremoniously, into the sink.

Later, Sally caught up with emails on the computer, while Granny Em planned her trip and Pamela looked through her own vast collection of digital photos, occasionally sharing a happy memory with Sally and Granny Em and sometimes just putting a picture aside that she might want to portray in oils one day.

Pamela was so absorbed in sorting images that both her daughter and mother-in-law went to bed – leaving her to carry on but expressing the hope that she wouldn't stay up too much longer.

Eventually, long after lights had gone out in both her daughter's bedroom and her mother-in-law's, Pamela found the photos from the Alicante Business Fair.

There were far too many to look at now, and anyway, she wanted Sally to see them with her so, whilst she was relieved to have found them, she was happy to leave browsing through them for another day.

Making sure that she had saved them again in her computer, where she could find them easily, she went to bed, feeling more positive about life in Spain with Sally, than she'd felt for a long while.

It was about ten-past-eight in the evening before Sofía arrived at the mortuary. Tuesday had already been an incredibly busy day and she was tired. Still, it was good that the Coroner was able to find a slot for the autopsy, so soon. Like the region's forensics teams, he too was being kept busy.

She found every mortuary to be a depressing place, chilling on so many levels, not least because the temperatures in the autopsy room were always kept below anything Sofía found comfortable.

By the time she'd scrubbed up and donned protective outer garments, latex gloves and a mask, the coroner had already begun his external examination.

"Ah, you are here, First Sergeant. Good, I want you to look at the knife in situ before I remove it"

Sofía walked up to the autopsy table. Egnacio was stretched out on his back, his clothes had been cut away and were bagged up on the nearby counter waiting for forensics. Only the cloth surrounding the knife remained; evidence might have been transferred to the material as the knife plunged in. The effect was rather bizarre.

Egnacio's scrawny, naked frame, glistening palely under the bright clinical lights, seemed to be pinned to the dull, scrubbed, clinically clean metal surface, under a bright orange patchwork square. All that was missing was a dripping Dali clock to finish the surreal effect.

The bloodied material around the entry wound would be removed at the same time as the knife – so that the blade was not drawn back through the shirt, 'cleaning' itself in the process. Instead, the knife and material would be bagged together, still attached.

"Ok, Gomez, I am looking, but apart from noting that the man had appalling taste in shirt colours, what am I looking at?" Sofía asked.

"The knife. It's an unusual choice of weapon – so was it brought to the scene, in which case it was a bizarre choice – or could it already have been there?"

Gomez gave her a few minutes to look at it more closely, then continued. "You will see more clearly when I pull out the blade, but I recognised what it is, from the handle. It's an antique, for a start. Before I remove it, you can see that the knife entered on the victim's left side. He would have been standing when he was stabbed. It's likely that the killer used his right hand to hold the knife. The blade is old and long, it would have taken a lot of strength and a few seconds to embed it as deeply as it is. The angle is slightly inclined upwards. I expect it to have pierced the heart, when I open him up, I will confirm."

Gomez mimicked the upward thrusting motion of the attack. "The indications are that, as he was stabbed with an upright thrust on his left side, the killer pressed him down onto the chair by pushing hard on his right shoulder. There is faint bruising already showing there," he pointed at the shoulder, "...indicating that it happened just before he died. The entry wound was ripped upwards as the knife was held stationary and the body was pushed downwards against the direction of the cut. Whoever did this was strong."

Sofía noted the point of entry and the angle of the blade. "Will that give us a rough idea of the assailant's height?" she questioned.

"Only roughly, the killer could have crouched, or been standing on something they later removed but Egnacio was five-feet-eight inches tall. It's likely that his killer was over five-feet-six and, probably, a similar height to the deceased. It's unlikely that he is over five-feet-ten inches but, however unlikely, it isn't impossible. So, don't dismiss a suspect based on height. It might, however, confirm the viability of a suspect, if they are around five-feet-eight. The killer must have used his hand to press down on the victim's shoulder. As the bruising becomes clearer, that should also give an indication of the killer's hand size and that will also help to determine their likely height."

They waited while the mortuary assistant took close-up photos of the knife sticking out of the body. "These will be used by the prosecution to confirm that the wound site is unchanged from when the body was first found." Sofía looked puzzled, until he added, "Basically, making sure that we haven't added any damage or changed the weapon's position by moving the body with the weapon in place."

The assistant moved away from the table once he was done and moved to a computer desk to confirm that the table's remotely operated autopsy camera was working. Fixed to the ceiling, it dangled like an upside-down 1960's anglepoise desk lamp, a little incongruous in the modern, bare sterile room.

Once he had the go-ahead that the digital video camera was on and OK, Gomez moved forward and slowly pulled out the blade. "I took the precaution of getting the body scanned, before we started, just in case the blade rips the flesh on exiting". As Gomez talked, Sofía watched, amazed. The small ivory coloured handle had given her no clue as to how long the blade would be. Sinuously wavy, the blade was nearly a foot long and, for all the world, looked like a wriggling snake that had been run over by a lawn roller.

"It is a south east Asian Kris, nineteenth century," Gomez informed her. "With the ivory handle and its case intact, it could be worth a couple of hundred euros, at least. I would suggest that you check with the forensic team and ask if they discovered a wooden sheath. If the killer improvised and grabbed the weapon on the spur of the moment, He might not have remembered to wipe his prints off the casing, even though they were certainly wiped off the handle of the kris".

Sofía made notes as Gomez talked. The rest of the autopsy was straightforward. The stomach contents and various blood and tissue samples were put to one side for tox screens and any other information they could reveal.

Before she left, she used her phone to take photos of the knife. Her next stop would be to re-examine the murder site and check with the crime scene technicians, to see if the scabbard had been found and whether the blade was listed on the shop inventory; it was an hour later however, before she managed to track it down. It was worth the effort, though, as it confirmed that the kris was listed as a stock item. This could well have been a crime of opportunity, rather than planned.

She needed to find the witnesses.

Chapter 10 – Sally's Wednesday Morning

Her mother was back working on the portrait, again, when Sally let herself out of the apartment. Granny Em was nowhere in evidence, so Sally assumed that she'd gone off for the day with her 'new' admirer. Sally decided to stay out for lunch and looked forward to seeing Lola again. There had been no time for a long chat since the murder, what with her gran and everything else.

Lola was sitting at one of her tables darning holes in a white cloth, it was still too early for lunch and the breakfast customers had finished and drifted away, so it was quiet in the café. She glanced up from her sewing and looked very happy to see Sally.

"What on earth are you doing, Lola?" Sally asked as she settled down on the chair next to the busy café owner. José came out of the kitchen and offered a glass of red wine to Sally then seeing the expression on Lola's face, turned smartly and went straight back into the kitchen. As she sipped, she commented, "José appears to be looking forward to getting back to college, rather than someone enjoying his holiday!"

Lola grimaced and gestured at the jagged tear she was working on. "The Guardia found my tablecloth while they were looking for the dog and the man! It was new for the summer season, so I'm not replacing it, I'm repairing."

"Ahh, so that's why José looks so guilty. The women who saw the accident said it wasn't his fault, Lola."

"Pfft, the crash may have been an accident, but he didn't need to ride off before untangling the cloth from the bike handle. It made the damage so much worse. He's now in the kitchen, where he has to work for me all week. No running off. His bike wheel isn't straight, it's wobbly and needs to be repaired, so he will have to walk to choir until he's earned the money to pay for it."

They chatted while Sally sipped her wine, keeping it well away from the tablecloth. Once she'd brought Lola up to date about everything that had happened since she'd found Egnacio López, Lola talked about the Guardia and told her all that she'd heard about their investigation.

Pedro was the main link to the Policía Local, but her boyfriend, Roberto was also helping between his shifts on Neighbourhood Patrol because the *Jefe*, the Chief Inspector, wanted to assist the Guardia in solving the murder before the main tourist season kicked in. The leading hotel had already had a few cancellations and he was worried. It could be bad for Summer trade if the murder wasn't solved quickly.

Lola mentioned the Sergeant, Sofía Gonzales, and admitted that she'd been a little jealous when she'd seen her Roberto running errands for his pretty boss. "She is *muy bonita*, yes? Beautiful – so you can guess how pleased I was when her husband came to collect her yesterday. He stopped off here to have coffee while he waited for her. He is very handsome, like her, and *ohhh Sally*, they have the sweetest little baby girl, he showed me photos on his phone, sooo sweet. I cannot think how she can part from the little girl, every day."

Lola then told her that Roberto was visiting vets and that the Guardia would be finished in the jewellery shop tomorrow, when Egnacio's son would be coming in to check the inventory and organise the return, to each owner, of jewellery left for repair. He'd already been in briefly, yesterday, to see if anything had been stolen during the murder, but they didn't think so. If there had been a theft, it wasn't obvious, but maybe the stock-take would show something missing.

Sally was secretly pleased that Sofía Gonzales was married, although she wouldn't face up to why. She didn't have time for a boyfriend. She needed to be there for her mother.

They chatted on for a while, speculating about whether the man with the dog would be found and if he was the murderer. Lola admitted that she really didn't like Egnacio's son very much and secretly hoped it would be him, so that Angelica could take the lease and expand her business.

Once the repair of the tablecloth was finished Sally noticed that the tables were starting to fill up with people eating lunch. The smell of fresh paella and grilled fish mingled with the smell of the sea, coffee and wine made her feel ravenous.

While Lola saw to the tables, Sally decided to be wicked and have *Magret de Pato* for lunch. She ordered another glass of wine, to drink while she was waiting for her duck. It might take a while for her memories of discovering Egnacio to fade, but this was a good way to start. She wondered, idly, what Pedro was doing, Lola hadn't said. No matter, she had her mother and gran to keep her amused for now.

Greg put down the menu that he'd used to screen his face and got up from the table. Sally sat facing away from him and, clearly, was totally absorbed in her thoughts. She would be there for a while, she'd just ordered food, so he had time to run a few errands. He'd give her half an hour to get her food and start eating; he would be back before she finished. Time then to decide if he was going to approach her or carry on following her.

Following her was entertaining. He was not the only predator in town, from the look of it. The murderer might yet be of use to him, so maybe he should wait before confronting Sally.

Chapter 11 – Pamela's Wednesday

Pamela saw the suspect list on the coffee table, when she went into the sitting room to open the shutters and let in some air. Sally had included all the people connected with the murder so far, it was quite comprehensive. Fancy that, her daughter was turning into an amateur sleuth. perhaps Sally was more interested in Pedro than she'd realised; she was clearly trying to impress '*someone*' with the list.

Pamela hadn't noticed it yesterday, but she'd been too absorbed collating photos. She was pleased with the pictures she'd found and hoped Sally would have time to look at them this morning, after breakfast.

She was surprised that her daughter was getting so involved, she hadn't been all that close to Egnacio, but finding someone's dead body must build a connection, she supposed... a sense of obligation, maybe?

Thinking about it over coffee, Pamela could appreciate that Sally found Pedro attractive and, even if he wasn't her only motivation for becoming involved, he was definitely icing on the cake!

It looked like a short list, but she hadn't known Egnacio that long. Pamela sipped her drink and, picking up the pen from the table, started adding the few people she knew who were likely to be pleased that Egnacio was no longer vying for trade along the beach front.

Angelica, at the dress shop between the Jeweller and Lola's had been trying to get the lease for Egnacio's for a while, in order to set up a workshop for local seamstresses.

Egnacio's son was always rowing with his father, so no love lost there, everyone knew that, but Egnacio's daughter-in-law was a very unpleasant woman. She'd never tried to be nice to Egnacio. Rumour had it that her mother and her father-in-law had fallen for each other when she was in her early teens. The break-up had been nasty, so she hated him for hurting her mother, even though that was how she and his son had met.

There were also rumours that Egnacio was acting as an unlicensed pawn shop, lending money on items he listed as 'repairs' then appropriating them before their due date, if a customer came in wanting to buy them.

She'd known the first, but not about items going missing until, only the other day, she overheard a woman in the *Correos* complain. Egnacio had sold her mother's crucifix, the day before the date the she'd arranged to pop in and pay back the loan. Pamela wondered if anyone in the Guardia had wondered why there were so many 'repairs' in the shop and so few that actually needed fixing. She must ask Pedro later.

Raoul had said he would be visiting, around supper time to share what he'd found out about Carlos.

She'd just added '*daughter-in-law, woman in post office and everyone in the repair list, whose items aren't there anymore*' to Sally's list together with the other names she'd already thought of, when Sally came through with more coffee.

Delighted that her mother was helping her sleuth, they went through the revised list together and agreed to hover near Raoul's door, around the time they expected Pedro to be leaving him. Maybe they could both be persuaded to enjoy a glass of wine.

Pamela switched on her laptop and opened the file where she'd stored the exhibition photos, while Sally gathered bowls, spoons, cereal and milk. It was already too bright outside to see the computer screen, so instead of breakfasting on the balcony, as they normally did, enjoying their discreet vantage point over the square and all its morning bustle, they decided to stay in the sitting room. The laptop screen was always brighter when plugged in, anyway.

The first few photos were of one or the other of Sally's parents enjoying the trade fair that they'd gone there to support. It was interesting, as Sally spotted a few local shop owners that she'd met since coming to live in the Port.

She was sure mother must have shown her some of the snaps before, but the hurt of seeing her father on the screen and not then knowing much about the townspeople, meant she hadn't paid much attention to what else was happening in each picture.

Going through the photos now, slowly, with her mother chatting about each one, was interesting. She knew so many more people now than she had before.

She saw a young Lola several times, in the background. In almost every shot of her, she was dragging a pre-teen José away from sweet and toy stalls, with two harassed looking parents lagging behind them.

In one of the general aisle views of busy stalls and happy people, she saw something odd, but wasn't sure what, so asked her mother to make a sub-folder to drop it in, to look at later.

The next set of photos showed the horse and equestrian events. They were good shots but, apart from her parents, contained no one she knew, so they didn't dwell on them.

Finally came the pageantry and drama of the costume fair. Pamela had taken a lot of photos, in case there were details she could use in paintings.

They sat, finishing breakfast as they flicked through the pictures, admiring the artistry of the costume designers.

"Wait, go back ...yes there. That stall holder was one of the women at Lola's! Younger, but I'm sure it was her! Can you put that in the save folder as well mother, please? Are there any more of her stall? I am sure I know the person she's talking to, but he's hidden by that black dress... Yes, there's another, you must have taken a shot back down the aisle before you went on to the next. It's Egnacio – she was talking to him and he is showing her something in a blue cloth jewellery bag, like those he used in the shop. I think he said they were impregnated with jeweller's rouge powder as it kept whatever was in them clean and shiny. How odd!" Sally leaned across and saved the photo with the other two, scanning through the last few shots quickly, to see if there were any more of interest.

The rest were just general shots of dresses and the last, an exquisite costume jewellery necklace, the one that her father had wanted to buy her mother, just before they had to dash back to the hotel.

On the other side of the port, in Café Mediteraneo, Mario wasn't completely happy with his new bookkeeper. He thought that maybe the English way of doing things wasn't as complicated as the Spanish way. She was either making it look too easy, or she wasn't getting it right.

His last admin clerk had made doing the paperwork look much more complicated, but then, that was his sister, she'd even made getting married complicated and had insisted on Valencia for everything except the honeymoon.

They were somewhere in the Azores for the next month – then perhaps she'd come back to the restaurant to help him.

Chapter 12 - Herbert's Wednesday

Herbert Loomis was tired, hungry and very worried. He couldn't lie low for much longer, he needed to get food. If only he had a car he could go shopping outside the Port. Although, if he did have a car, he could try driving home. But, with no money, he couldn't even get petrol to go for food let alone buy it when he got to the shop. It all boiled down to money and that was what he was missing thanks to that stupid old man.

He opened the shutter just enough to see down the street and check that there were no Guardia bearing down on him, then closed it quickly, before he could be seen by prying neighbours.

He hated the Port; he hated his life and he hated the inevitability of everything that had happened to him that week.

If he hadn't put all his money on a straight that night...

If he'd registered that three of the cards on the table were hearts so there was a strong chance the other player had a flush...

If he hadn't carried on playing using IOUs...

If he'd won, instead of losing as badly and humiliatingly as he did...

If he hadn't stolen the brooch from Frau Schmeckler, after she'd been kind enough to give him a job...

If he hadn't pawned the brooch to Egnacio to clear his debt...

If Egnacio hadn't lied and said he'd sold the brooch, before he'd had a chance to retrieve it and sneak it back into the Schmeckler house...

If wishes were horses, he would have several getaway options quietly neighing in his back garden by now!

Those women, they worried him.

He'd seen them staring at the shop entrance, as he ran out. He'd looked straight into the eyes of the Spanish one, as he stumbled through the doorway, it was that look that haunted him now, a cruel, knowing look. Even in his panic, he'd sensed a predator and it was that second of distraction, when he was already afraid, that had caused him to crash with Fritz into the boy on the bike! They might otherwise have made a clean getaway.

That much drama on the street though, must have been seen, and he knew he must have been recognised. If he had, it was his own fault. He'd been walking Fritz down that way most of the week, while he tried to work out how to get his life back together.

Walking past Egnacio's every day had been his way of reminding himself that he'd made his own mess. He must get help for his gambling addiction once he got the brooch back and found a way to get home. Home. It took being stranded in another country to make him realise how much he'd had.

He was sure the women had followed him. He'd seen one, hovering near the top of the Calle two days in a row.

He'd been so angry that, the second time, he'd rushed out into the street to confront her, but there had been no sign of her when he got to the junction. Then he'd realised that, out of the house, he was too exposed and vulnerable so had gone back in, as quickly as he could. Even though there was rarely anyone around at that time of day – he could take no risks.

He didn't know what he was going to do, his passport had expired last month, he hadn't had the money to get a new one and he hadn't wanted anyone in the UK to know where he was. His job seeker's allowance had stopped, as he wasn't turning up to collect it, and, of course, he had run out of credit on his phone. Maybe he could still find a way to ring them and try bluffing his way into getting the money.

He couldn't understand it. His mates who were on social seemed to spend more time in Benidorm than they did in the UK, and none of them seemed to be penniless. He was doing something wrong. There was some trick they knew that he didn't understand. Maybe friends in the UK signed on for them? He didn't know, it was all too much, he wanted to go home and now he couldn't.

This wasn't living the dream, this was being frightened, alone, tired, constantly poor and hungry. Now, this business with Egnacio, those women, the Guardia!

He just didn't know what he was going to do.

But he needed to start by getting food.

Before the villa owner's elderly TV had packed up, he'd seen a programme about people who found ways of recycling food from supermarket and restaurant waste. Maybe he would have a late-night poke about in the bins behind café Mediterraneo, after they closed for business tonight. He'd find food before it went off in the heat and before the stray cats and rats found it. Not a pleasant prospect, but it would be a change from street watching.

He decided that he might as well siesta.

He should be safe here.

This wasn't the address that he'd given Fritz's owner, it wasn't even in the same part of town, so it was unlikely that they'd find him.

He was just being silly.

The owners of this house weren't due to return until next month, he'd seen the letter from their internet provider confirming the dates when they wanted it turned back on. So, first food, then get out of Puerto Amarillo, sell the brooch he'd picked up from Egnacio's counter and work out how to get back to the UK with no passport.

It was a pity that the refugee encampments had been closed in Northern France, he might have been able to get back that way. If he'd been in Spain, legitimately, he could have talked to the British Embassy, he was pretty sure there was a Consulate office in Alicante. Not going to happen though, he had made too many mistakes and wasn't going to risk losing his benefit for good. Once home, he could apply for a replacement passport anytime but, more importantly he could sign back on. In any event, one thing he was sure about, no matter how much fun it looked in his aunt's *chick flick* books, he wasn't going to be putting Dog Walker on his CV.

Chapter 13 – Wednesday Evening

Pamela and Sally were unsure what their discoveries meant, but they knew it was important that they show Pedro.

It wasn't just because it might help to identify one of the witnesses, there was something about the way that Egnacio and the stall holder had been interacting that suggested there was something fishy about whatever they were doing.

Sally went to fetch her mobile phone from her handbag and only heard Pedro and Raoul outside the apartment because she'd left the front door of the apartment slightly ajar in case Granny Em decided to return early. It was as well the door wasn't shut, she thought, or else she wouldn't have heard anything, and they would have missed him altogether.

Sally opened the door wide as soon as she heard Raoul say goodbye and go back inside his apartment. Pedro was turning to leave so she called out to him. From Raoul's demeanour, it was obvious that whatever Pedro had found out about Carlos, hadn't made him happy.

Pedro looked pleased to be invited in for a glass of wine and was happy to join them on the balcony. There was a light breeze, but it was still warm, even though the sun was now mellowing, ready for sunset.

Once the bottle was opened and the glasses filled,

Sally explained what they'd discovered.

"The photos were taken six years ago but I'm sure that woman on the costume stall, talking to Egnacio, is one of the women I saw in Lola's. We thought it might be important because, until now, I'd thought they were both tourists and new to the Puerto. Is it important, do you think?"

Sally barely paused before thrusting the other printout at Pedro. "I saw something in this photo too, but can't be sure, as the only time I saw the dog it was running away – but could this be the same one?"

Pedro was mesmerised. Frau Schmeckler, her dog, Marianne Thompson and Egnacio walking together in the aisle of the Exhibition Hall, in what looked like friendly conversation and then the other photo, Egnacio and a woman, not the one he'd met, but presumably Valentina Karkoff, all at the same event.

This was six years ago but they were all connected to Egnacio in some way.

Marianne claimed to have only just met Valentina, but it seemed that might not be true.

"Thank you Sally. And Pamela, these photos are amazing. Did you recognise anyone else in them?"

Pamela replied straight away. "Well yes, there was a whole contingent of shop owners and crafts people from the Port – it was a big event for the region, to promote some of the small towns to tourists. I expect the Exhibition centre will still have a full list of the stand holders for all the events that were on that week and they might be able to give you more information."

Pedro first asked if they could email digital versions of the photos they had picked, then he thought about it more and asked if he could have copies of all the photos taken that day – even the equestrian shots, in case there was anything else in the background that might help to connect the witnesses to Egnacio.

Quietly, he sipped his wine and listened to Sally and Pamela chatting about people in the other photos. He ran through in his head everything he could remember from Marianne's interview.

It wasn't reliable without playing his recording or looking at his notes, neither of which he could do here, even if he wanted to.

However, he couldn't remember Marianne saying anything indicating that she knew Egnacio at all. Now there she was! Not only talking to Egnacio, but also to Frau Schmeckler.

Maybe she wasn't just a witness. Sally was sure that Marianne had been sitting there for a while before the dog collided with José's bike, but nobody had asked Lola when the women arrived.

Lola had also been at the Exhibition, so another reason to chat with her. He could show her the photos, and ask if she had taken any herself, or could remember anything.

At least Roberto's girlfriend wasn't even remotely near the Guardia's ever widening radar, as she'd been up to her ears in customers when the man had burst out of the shop...

But that was also a puzzle because the autopsy report, although not complete, suggested the possibility that Egnacio could have been dead for between one and two hours before the Guardia arrived.

Surely, if the door of the shop had been wide open for longer, it would have been noticed sooner?

He could still have died just before the man and dog fled. It was within the timeframe, but Sally had described the red liquid on the doorstep as looking like the residue of sticky red wine – so presumably someone in Forensics was working out the blood's drying rate according to the weather report that day, maybe that was one of the lab tests still being done.

Pamela interrupted his thoughts by offering him another refill.

She cleared her throat. "Pedro, there is something else you should know about Egnacio, you might want to take a very good look at the repair list... Egnacio's eyes weren't as good as they used to be. He stopped doing repairs in the shop, he sent them away, so the ones he kept in the shop are unlikely to be in need of fixing."

"I've never heard this before, Pamela. Surely, being on Neighbourhood Patrol, this is something I would have known?"

"Well, setting up as a pawn shop without a licence and without declaring the loans and interest payments to the Hacienda is probably not legal here – any more than it would be in the UK." Pamela sighed, "I would never have known, if I hadn't needed to borrow money for my husband's funeral. In Spain, as you know, once the death is announced, a deceased's assets are frozen until probate is cleared. Bills for the funeral and taxes etcetera must be paid, before you can inherit, and everything is released. I only needed a bridging loan, but the bank wasn't helpful, whereas, when I took some jewellery into

Egnacio to get it appraised he was very kind. He lent me the money for the funeral, but when everything was sorted and I went back, he seemed sad to let me have all the pieces back." Then Pamela repeated the conversation she'd heard in the Post office and how upset the woman was, not to have had her crucifix returned.

Sally leaned back, in the warm sunshine, watching her mother and Pedro interact, this felt right, the way it should be. She imagined Pedro turning to her with those mesmerising eyes and murmuring something loving and affectionate to her in that throaty sexy voice...

Whoa, where did that come from?

Shaking her head to rid it of images of the two of them, on a quiet Mediterranean beach, in a deep passionate embrace, she sighed. Nope, never, not happening. *Not happening!* She caught her mother eyeing her and could feel her face going red, just as Pedro turned his decidedly mesmerising eyes and looked straight at her, through her even... no, he was looking behind her, through the sitting room into Pamela's studio.

His seat was just angled in the perfect place to see between the bookshelves that artificially screened it from the rest of the room – and he'd obviously just noticed the sparkling dress.

She gulped, partly relieved that he wasn't noticing her embarrassment but also miffed that he wasn't looking at her at all. As if reading her thoughts, he turned to her and gave her such an intense look that she had difficulty breathing.

"*Ahh mi Cariña, debemos posponer nuestro tiempo juntos un poco más,*" he breathed quietly into her ear as he stood, leaning forward across the table, ostensibly to take a better look at the dress. Then he turned to her mother, "Pamela, you will show me your studio, please? I am interested in seeing Senorita Garcia's dress for the fiesta – and your painting, if I may? It *is* the costume for la Reina, *si*?"

Pamela was pleased to show him the costume, but was a little worried when he got out his phone and started taking photos of the dress and the intricate bodice work. "Please, Pedro, don't do that, I have been trusted with the dress, because of the portrait and because they know I will not show anyone in the town. The dress. It was made especially for Sofía and nobody is meant to see it until the first event when she wears it. It was very expensive and must be kept secret."

"Who made it, do you know?"

"It was that new dressmaker from Madrid. I'm sorry, I don't know her name. Apparently, it is so special that some of the fabric and crystals originated in Argentina. She has even arranged to buy it back when the fiesta is over, so that she can dismantle it; no one else can ever duplicate this design. Señor Garcia is delighted about this – so much so that he helped her by getting all the orders she sent for costume jewellery and fabric, for this and several other dresses, through all the documentation and customs procedures, using his family connections. It is saving him over a thousand euros on the dress, having her buy it back, later – but you must NOT tell anyone Pedro, unless it's police business."

Pamela looked at him very sternly with what, had he known it, was the special look normally reserved for Sally when she wasn't being a good daughter. "I'm only telling you all this because you obviously think it's important. I don't want to sound silly and secretive if the Police really need to know, but please, don't tell anyone else. I have to LIVE here!"

Pedro understood and promised that it would go no further than his sergeant, unless the Guardia felt it was relevant to their investigation.

He felt guilty, he was talking as if he didn't think that anyone would need to know, but if he was right, everyone would know soon. The connections and coincidences were too much to be happenstance. Apologising, he turned away from her to text Sofía. While he waited to see if the sergeant had seen his message. Pamela moved back into the sitting room, sensing that he needed a moment, alone, to think. Staring out of the window, while he worked through some likely scenarios that included the painting, his eyes were drawn to the street at the edge of the square. There was a minor kerfuffle going on, as a minibus tried to mow down a pedestrian under the pretext of pulling off the road. The man on the pavement had been weaving his way down the street, a little drunk and not paying attention where he walked. The bus-driver was clearly unimpressed and aggrieved that he had tried to lurch under his wheels. As they vocalised their grievances and a crowd with conflicting opinions gathered around to discuss, noisily, who was at fault, Pedro saw Carlos getting out of the back of the minibus and walk behind it, away from the dispute – completely out of sight of his own flat. He looked, furtively, up and down the road, before shouldering his overnight bag and walking away..

Pedro was just about to call out to Sally and Pamela that Carlos was back early, for a change, when, instead of heading towards them and his apartment, Carlos darted into a side street on the other side of the square.

Consumed with curiosity and concern for his two friends, Pedro made rapid excuses to Pamela and Sally and almost ran from the apartment.

"Bother, I was just about to suggest that you invited him to supper, Sally, the quickest way to a man's heart is the discovery that you are a good cook!"

Pamela grinned at Sally's fleeting expressions of horror and relief, that there hadn't been time – then wondered if she should translate Pedro's murmured Spanish to Sally. *'Darling, we must postpone our time together a little more'* So romantic ...but she mustn't, she wasn't supposed to have heard, so maybe not, unless Sally asked. Plus, having a local boyfriend whose endearments were in his own tongue would be a huge incentive for Sally to learn Spanish. Mmm, she must fish out some of the recipe books she'd used when she first came here. The first thing that Sally must learn how to make, in the Valencian region, was paella.

She made a mental note to find out more about Pedro's family tomorrow but, for now, supper.

Half-an-hour later, she and Sally settled down to a pizza sent up from the restaurant below and an evening of Ealing comedy repeats on TV.

Granny Em came in, just before bedtime, with another bouquet of flowers and some salty tales about older men and how they never changed, even though their years advanced.

Pedro managed to get to the corner of the square just in time to see Carlos going into Alexandro's, a new jewellery store that had only opened about six months ago. It didn't stock traditional jewellery like the stuff that Egnacio had, they were more up to date, a small independent shop modelled on one of the new chains of ultra-modern jewellery stores springing up all over Spain.

Typically, it stocked a few modern, blingy, overpriced gold and platinum rings and necklaces, but most of the display window was full of middle-of-the-road watches, only marginally better than the eight-euro variety sold by Chinese supermarkets, but much more expensive.

He expected that they, at least, would not be sorry to see Egnacio's business closed. They would be glad of one less competitor for the tourist trade.

Pedro watched from the corner of the Post Office building; Carlos was barely in the shop for more than a few minutes. Closing the door behind him, he turned right as he left the jeweller and walked a few yards to gaze at the offers in a Travel Agent's window. He glanced up and down the narrow street, obviously checking that he wasn't being watched, then went in.

Pedro waited a little while, but felt it was wrong to stalk Carlos like this. It was clear that he was up to something, but Pedro knew how much Carlos loved

Raoul, so he refused to think that there was anything bad going on, even though it was odd. Maybe Carlos needed to know how much he was upsetting his partner. However, Pedro checked his watch, it wasn't going to be tonight. First, he needed to catch the sergeant and pass on the photos with his theory and then home to Cha-Cha who would be hungry by now and very bored cooped up in the yard, even if it was enclosed, cool and shady with fresh water. She would want a run. Podencos were dogs that were designed to run and hunt hares, not snooze all day. He wondered if Sally and Cha-Cha would like each other when they met. He hoped so; you can tell a lot about people from how they interact with your dog.

Greg moved away from the restaurant under Sally's apartment, scowling as he walked towards the Pedro-boyfriend lurking at the corner of the Correos, in front of him.

Before Greg could confront him, the policeman looked at his watch, then walked swiftly to his car. Greg changed direction smoothly, in case there were any onlookers on Sally's balcony. There was no need to make his interest in Sally and her new life too obvious. He needed to be very careful, he'd seen Emma waving a camera around, indiscriminately snapping everything around her, silly old bat. The last thing he needed was for Emma to take a picture of him and ruin his *surprise*. He'd have to keep a low profile and stay out of Sally's way, for now. There'd be plenty of time to make the bitch suffer, the longer it took, the longer he'd have to enjoy it.

Chapter 14 – Two A.M Thursday

Herbert made sure all the lights in the house were off, before slipping out of the front door, locking it behind him. The street was quiet, as normal, not even the local cats were in evidence as he passed a favourite feline meeting place. A few minutes later he was staring at a shuttered Café Mediterraneo.

The main part of the restaurant was dark and unlit. It was closed and looked as if the staff had all gone. Herbert edged down the side passage that led to the back of the café. He didn't notice the glimmer in the manager's office, or the flickering light, which indicated that someone was still there, he was too interested in what might have been disposed of in the large skip he could see on the other side of the railing.

With only one obstacle left between him and food. His clambering over the fence was neither elegant, nor quiet.

The torch was weak, but it was strong enough to see a half lettuce and a plastic bag of tomatoes that were past their best but looked edible. Underneath, in another bag, was the end of an Ibérico ham with a good deal of scrappy meat left on it.

Finally, something good was happening to him!

He lifted the bags out of the bin, putting them into the basket he'd brought with him from the house, then he shone the torch back into the bin and screamed and screamed and screamed...

He was still shaking and screaming when the Police arrived thirty minutes later, by which time the restaurant really was empty. The office was as dead and still as the woman staring up out of the waste skip, just a lot less bloody.

By seven o'clock, Herbert was feeling much better. It had helped greatly that, once he'd been booked into a cell, given clean clothes and stripped of his remaining meagre possessions, he was given a cup of hot chocolate and a cheese and tomato tostado.

He'd never thought anything so simple as toast, with no butter, could taste so nice, but then – he'd never been hungry enough to go through a skip before.

Shuddering, he pushed that thought away. He didn't want to think about what forensic evidence they would get off his clothes. They'd treated him kindly, organised a solicitor and had rung the British Embassy, who'd sent a representative from Alicante, to see him.

They'd all been so gentle with him that he'd burst into the first real set of tears he'd shed, since the frustration of discovering his passport had run out. Only this wasn't frustration, this was relief, one way or another, it was over. Nothing that happened next could be as bad as this last week, nothing!

Both the solicitor and the woman from the Embassy had said pretty much the same thing. Once he'd earnestly denied killing either the old man or the woman in the skip – and admitted that he was hiding and had stolen because of being trapped in Spain, illegal and desperate, they both urged him to be open with the police.

Whatever petty crimes he'd committed, it would be better to tell the truth, so it could be faced and dealt with, rather than risk being put in prison for either of the murders, let alone for both.

He hadn't really needed much persuading. The hot drink, food and the promise from the embassy that, as soon as he'd faced whatever punishment Spain elected to serve him, they would do their best to sort out his passport disaster (and try to get him home) was the clincher. It all meant that, contrary to the fears instilled by English papers about Spanish jails, for the first time in a month he felt safe.

It was crazy, but a relief, no worries about food tomorrow, he would have a dry bed tonight and no more bodies!

Sofía had a hard job keeping up with his statement. The week's events spewed out of him so fast that even the Scot from the British Embassy, who was sitting in the preliminary interviews as a courtesy, had to ask him to slow down.

Eventually, they got the story of his horrible, *horrible*, last few weeks.

The passport wasn't even the start. He only discovered that the passport had expired after he decided to go home to the UK. He made that decision after losing his rented flat, as he'd run out of money. That happened because he lost his job in the beach bar for drinking the bar profits and that had been because he lost his girlfriend who was tired of being the one on the better wage who paid for their night's out and their meals at the Indian.

All in all, living the dream with no planning or money or decent job prospects and limited Spanish had lost its attraction when he was hungry with no bed for the night.

He'd got the job as a dog walker because his ex had found it for him through her new boyfriend, a waiter from the Indian restaurant.

Frau Schmeckler was odd, but she spoke great English. She was always very clear about what time he should return and paid him every day when he brought Fritz back.

Then one day he'd been early. The battery on his watch had run out and he'd had to guess the time.

He'd been surprised to find the kitchen door open, but it meant that he could take Fritz straight in. If anything, he assumed that she'd left it that way for him.

Frau Schmeckler was talking to at least two other women in the lounge. He couldn't see them, but he could hear that they were arguing about something and decided not to interrupt, especially as he'd no idea what they were saying. They were not speaking English.

He closed the kitchen door, quietly, and went to sort out some water for Fritz. As he opened the fridge door to get Fritz's special bottled water out for the bowl, a blue cloth bag fell from where it was resting on top of the fridge, spilling its contents on the floor.

As he picked the brooch up, putting it back into the bag, he couldn't help noticing how beautiful it was. Ten clear crystals surrounded a slightly larger one that reflected the light prettily. It probably wasn't worth much, or why would it be sitting there, on top of the kitchen fridge?

There was a good chance that Frau Schmeckler wouldn't even miss it for just a week. He could pawn it for week, so he could eat properly for a few days, and then, if he managed to get a couple of the odd jobs he'd been offered, he could retrieve it and smuggle it back into the Frau's villa.

That had been the plan. He'd popped the bag into his pocket and left the villa, as quietly as he'd entered. He walked the dog up and down the road for a few minutes, then made a big noise, ringing the front door and chatting to the dog, loudly, as if he'd just arrived. Within an hour, he was at Egnacio's and had arranged to pawn the brooch for a hundred euros. He suspected that it was worth an awful lot more, but he hadn't liked the look on Egnacio's face. He thought there was a strong chance that the brooch had been recognised so he just took the hundred to pay back a gambling debt and, with the change, buy his first decent meal in days.

Wandering around the town, later that evening, he'd found an empty house, which still had the electricity turned on and running water. That night he'd moved in.

Walking Fritz near the jeweller's shop, every day, had been his way of reminding himself that he had to get the brooch back and return it to the Frau's kitchen. He didn't think she'd noticed it was missing; if she had, she hadn't said anything. Ironically, it was the job of walking the Frau's dog that had earned him enough money to get the jewellery back, that last day.

He'd gone into the shop to pay off the loan and get back the brooch. Yes, the door had been open, but he didn't notice until he got right up to it and saw it slightly ajar.

He'd pushed his way in and saw the brooch lying on the counter. As he walked across to pick it up, popping it back into the blue bag lying next to it, the dog had whimpered and pulled on its lead. It was then he'd noticed Egnacio sitting, silently, on the chair, apparently asleep. Herbert's sleeve had brushed into wet blood as he leaned across to poke Egnacio awake – not realising, until he touched him and his eyes had adjusted a little more, that there was a knife handle sticking out of the seated man, who was dead. Pulling hard on the leash, the dog made their next move for them. In complete agreement, they bolted from the shop, then Fritz had bowled the pair of them into the bike.

Herbert ran all the way back to the Schmeckler' house and jabbered something incoherent at the Frau. He couldn't remember what! And, after thrusting both brooch and dog at the woman, he ran all the way back to the house he was squatting in.

Sofía was pleased, his story tallied with what they'd guessed, except that Frau Schmeckler hadn't mentioned either the theft or the return of the brooch.

"Did you recognise anyone in the café, near Egnacio's, when you left?" She asked him.

"I'm not sure, there were two women, they were both staring at me as I ran out. I only glimpsed them for a few seconds, but one of them looked straight at me – like she knew me – and was expecting me to be there. She looked nasty. The other – I can't be sure, but I think she was the woman who came looking for me, the other day. She might even have been the woman in the skip, but I didn't do it, I really didn't…"

The rest of the interview was about his discovery of the second body.

Before they took him back to the cells and decided what they would do with him, Sofía made sure that he was given a decent lunch and a hot coffee. She believed him. It was too ridiculous a story, not to be true.

Tired and feeling weary, she headed back to the restaurant to check in with the forensic team.

Chapter 15 – Sally's Thursday Morning

The Charity Shop was buzzing with news, when Sally called in on her way down to Lola's.

They'd seen the Guardia swarming all over the restaurant when they'd opened up the book shop that morning and the police were still there now.

Gossip had decided that Mario was helping the Guardia with their enquiries, but everyone knew that whatever had happened to the woman, whoever she was, it was nothing to do with Mario.

He was born and raised in Puerto Amarillo – everyone knew him and everyone knew that he was too soft to kill anything bigger than a chicken and he struggled with that, leaving that side of the restaurant to his chef and his butcher.

But who knew her, whoever she was in the skip – and the man who they'd found with her, gibbering and screaming, as the police took him away?

He must have been starving, to have been going through the skip like that.

Was it really possible that he'd killed Egnacio, that he was this missing, mad British man? Whether in Spanish, German, French or English, the rumours were flying around the town.

"Oooh, Sally, Pedro is looking for you – he said, if you came in, to ask you to go up to the Café, he wants to show you some pictures to see if you recognise anyone, he said – nothing gruesome, but he can't get away for a bit." Louise was so pleased to pass on such an important message that she almost skipped.

"Isn't it dreadful though? We'd just decided that we would be eating there once a week, on their senior specials' day. I know that Mario has been released for now, but I don't know that we want to go there if they murder customers."

Everyone in the shop had a theory and it felt like everyone from the port was in the shop expressing it – probably because the shop window gave such a good view of the restaurant and all the forensic activity. What was worse is that they were expressing it in a lot of different languages, and nobody was being quiet or subdued – after all, it wasn't a library.

Harry took refuge behind the till where, sadly for the charity shop's finances, he was largely undisturbed. The gossipers weren't even pretending to browse or buy.

He nodded to Sally and asked her if she wanted him to come with her – in case the pictures *were* gruesome.

She smiled gratefully, at least she knew Harry well enough to it know that it wasn't prurient interest that motivated the offer, but genuine concern.

"No Harry. Thanks, but I will be fine. I'm sure Pedro wouldn't show me anything awful and that sergeant seems nice, so I don't think she would either. If I can help find who killed Egnacio, I should…" *Assuming the two murders were related*, she added to herself. She left the charity shop and headed up the hill towards the café.

As she walked, she couldn't help wondering if the man with the dog was the person led screaming from the café last night – why would he want to draw so much attention to himself and if he wasn't the murderer, how unlucky must he be? In barely a week, he had found both of the Port's only murder victims in at least ten years and the ten-year-old crime, she'd read about in the local paper, had been a domestic row that went horribly wrong, not violent murders like these.

When she got to the restaurant, she saw that it was Roberto on duty, on the edge of the crime scene. He was busy shooing curious pedestrians away from the forensic team, currently working on the restaurant's main doors and locks.

"Hola Senorita Sally, I will call the First Sergeant to come out to you. You don't want to go in there. She is expecting you." Roberto's entering the café was swiftly followed by his reappearance with the Guardia Sergeant, who looked tired.

With Roberto's help, Sofía set up a small table and a couple of chairs, away from the street in the welcome shade of the side passage. It was a useful place for her to gather her thoughts and to use her phone, away from the noise inside and the traffic on the street. It was also a perfect place to interview Sally. Roberto needed to be off on his rounds, soon, so she let him go while she checked her phone for messages. It was a relief to get rid of him, there was something about the way he lurked that made her feel uncomfortable.

Always Right

Pedro had emailed the exhibition photos with his suspicions about the dress, so she wanted to chat with Pamela too, but talking to Sally first was going to help break the ice later, and there was much that she wanted to discuss with Sally. She seemed to be one of the few co-operative witnesses in this investigation.

Unlike Roberto, Pedro was very good at his job, he'd done well to develop an association with Sally, it was surprising how much of a help the English girl was being. Was that too much of a good thing or just good luck?

Sofía watched her settling into her seat, trying to contain her sudden suspicion that maybe Sally was being too helpful. Then Pedro came out to join them, as she'd asked him to, in case she struggled with translating.

They were quite transparent this pair, they clearly liked each other, the atmosphere around them was almost electric. Maybe there was nothing wrong with Sally's helpfulness, after all.

They made a nice couple, both tall, both attractive and both intensely intelligent. At least it cleared the air for her.

"Thank you for coming here, we are so busy today, we are sorry that neither of us could come to you." Sofía started the interview with an apology while Pedro set his phone to record and set it on the table. "To begin, we have some photos to show you and we need to know if you recognise these people."

She pulled a tablet out of her briefcase and, having logged in, flicked through her photos until she reached those she wanted. She started with several they'd taken of Herbert Loomis last night, at the Station, when they'd booked him in. Although Sally was not a witness to the bike incident, there was always a chance that she might know something about him and, maybe, had seen him elsewhere. They were both British and the Port wasn't that big. At this point, any information they could get to fill in background detail would be good.

"Yes, I've seen him before – who is he? He goes to the Correos quite often, then sits in the square as near to the café as he can get, I'm pretty sure he uses their free customer wi-fi, as he always gets his phone out and fiddles with it. I just assumed he was playing internet games and catching up with friends. I have seen him several times a week since the start of Summer, enough to notice him, anyway. He often arrives around the time I have mid-morning coffee on the balcony but never buys anything from the café," was Sally's surprising response. "He hasn't been there all this week. Was he the man with the dog? I don't think I've ever seen him with a dog! I had no idea! He always wears a T-shirt and tracksuit bottoms; I don't think he has brought much of a wardrobe with him. I am sure it's the same man, that T-shirt is too distinctive and how many people looking like him wear the same T-shirt celebrating a defunct 1980's pop group, even if they were iconic?"

Sofía didn't nod, not that she really needed to, Sally was right, but there were enough rumours flying around, without adding any more. Pedro would need to go around the town centre with Roberto later and use their local contacts to check out who else had seen him and what he was up to.

Maybe there was someone in the Correos who would remember him and, because he was regular, perhaps they would know why he went there, what he did and who he knew?

Sally told them all she knew about Herbert, which was little more than she'd first said, apart from his always coming into the square walking towards the apartment, from the opposite side.

Sofía changed photos. This one wouldn't be such a nice one to look at.

"I am sorry Sally, but I need to show you a photo of the woman who was killed last night. It's not nice to look at photos of dead people and for reasons you do not want to know, I can only show you her profile, not her full face, but I hope that this is enough?" Sofía passed her the cleanest photo they'd got of the victim's face. It was almost as if she was in deep thought staring off into the distance, except the eyes were expressionless, as was the side of the face that was shown.

Sally looked at it very carefully, "I think she was the companion, the one the woman was talking to when they saw the accident. But I think I've seen her somewhere else too, in a photo, but a bit younger: one of those I gave you yesterday, I think. Have you shown Lola? She might be able to confirm it."

Sofía thanked her and said that they would be talking to Lola later, after Roberto was finished for the evening, so that he could sit in when she was interviewed. Lola had asked if he could be there and as she wasn't a suspect, there was no reason why he should not be.

Sally continued. "I wonder why she was killed. It

was her friend who was the main witness All this woman did, was be there at the same time, just as Lola, the Germans and everyone else in the café was that day, including me."

She paused, thinking aloud. "It all seems very odd to me. Maybe the two crimes are not connected," she continued, thoughtfully, "...except that the photos show she knew Egnacio – but then, I knew Egnacio. Lots of people knew Egnacio!" Sally was sure that there must be some significance in the fact that all the main people connected, even loosely, with Egnacio's death, apart from the man they'd now found, had been at the event her parents had attended in Alicante. Even if she couldn't see the connection, there must be one.

"Perhaps you need to come and talk to mother again, about the exhibition. She said, this morning, that she was going to see if she could find the old phone and my father's camera. She thinks they are still somewhere around, and he barely used them after that weekend, he got ill too fast. So, any photos that he took when he was alone at the fair, will be on them – mother was too upset to even think about looking at anything after he died, but she knows that she didn't throw them away. If she hasn't found them, when I get home, I'll look in all the places she can't reach."

Sofía was pleased that there was a chance of more photos, but she was even more pleased to have an excuse to visit and get more information out of Pamela, without making it a formal interview.

She also wanted to see the dress. Yes, she very much wanted to have a proper look at the dress, without making it too obvious to either Pamela or Sally. Not because she didn't trust them – oddly, she did. It was more about being concerned that showing too much interest in the dress might put both women in danger.

Whatever the police did next, they had to make sure that there were no more killings. Setting aside her civic duty and her natural concern, a selfish part of her was also aware that, as a First Sergeant, she had been lucky to be able to run with a case like this. Had so many senior officers not been looking at incidents in Barcelona this week, she would have had to work with an Inspector checking her every action.

She needed this case to be solved and she needed it done with minimal fuss. "Perhaps we can pop in to see you, after the restaurant is cleared, unless you don't mind waiting. It shouldn't be too much longer. We've said that Mario can re-open, now that he's been cleared of any involvement, so we need to be gone in the next hour, if not sooner, or else he won't be able to open this evening. His yard will be out-of-bounds for a few more days. He'll need to put smaller bins in the passageway for now. At least it means we can go back, later, to the station's air conditioning and wi-fi." Sofía smiled at the anticipation of having a desk, again, for a while.

She would need her laptop, too, to look through Pamela's photos in detail. They had been sent to the media department to be put through facial recognition software, but it wasn't the same as looking herself. The software might find people, but it didn't recognise atmosphere – and that might be important, if she was right.

Chapter 16 – Harry and Louise's Morning

Louise was cross, they had been so close to being involved in a real-life murder mystery and now the police were just ignoring them.

Harry was no help, he was just sitting at the counter again, reading a book and ignoring everything except the occasional genuine customer who actually wanted to buy a book. The place was still heaving with gossipers and locals taking advantage of their unparalleled view of the police working in and around the restaurant and, to cap it all, Sally had been sought out, ushered to a seat and was probably chatting happily away to the lead investigator, just out of sight.

Life wasn't fair, she and Harry had pointed the police at the restaurant, so why weren't they being interviewed.

The last straw was when Roberto stuck his head around the door to ask some of their genuine customers to leave as the shop had exceeded its health, safety and fire limits on the number of people allowed in the shop at once.

Still, it was easy to grab the bull by the horns, when he came into the shop, properly, to answer a question from Harry. "So, Roberto, have they released the name of whoever was found in the skip?"

Always Right

"Sorry Harry, you know I can't speak about an investigation. While I am here, can I ask you about the books you have in the shop? Do you have any, in Spanish, about travel?"

Louise was delighted to be able to help and, grabbing his arm, dragged him into the dark recesses of the shop, away from the window and the milling throng. She didn't care that Harry looked aghast after them or that Roberto tried to resist!

As they receded, there was a murmur of appreciation from the more vocal of the throng and she was sure she heard someone muttering, "Oooh, look at that, Lou has grabbed herself a toy boy right under Harry's nose!"

Unfortunately, she also heard the excited response. "Does that mean Harry might be free for supper and maybe something else?"

She stopped in mid-drag and looked round to cast a general frown in the direction of four beady eyes belonging to two well-known predatory widows - two eyes were following her movements whilst the other two were trying to get Harry's attention.

She pointed at a set of bookshelves. "These three shelves are all travel books. ...by the way, we saw you taking Sally to the Guardia sergeant in the alley, can you tell us anything about the murders?"

"You would make a good detective, but no, I cannot tell you that the woman was the one you saw and I may not tell you that we might have already found her murderer and the killer of Egnacio the jeweller!" Roberto winked at her as he started to work his way along the first shelf.

He knew that with that much information, she

would go away and leave him in peace to plan his much-anticipated holiday.

As expected, Louise turned and, armed with her exciting news, dashed to Harry's side just in time to deflect the two rapacious pensioners bearing down on him, as he froze near the till, transfixed in fear.

Once Roberto was alone and out of sight, he fished out the list of suggested destinations he'd been given and started to wade through the shelves.

It was a clever idea of hers, coming here, if anyone was curious about where they had gone, this is the last place they would expect a Spaniard to seek information.

Still, it wouldn't hurt to lay a few false trails, so he picked a book about Peruvian ancient monuments, one about exploring Egypt and the third, a travel guide to Caracas. All were in Spanish and were a bargain at less than five euros for them all. He paid Harry, who wasn't paying attention to anything apart from the converging women, and popped the books into his holdall. Roberto had errands to run and needed to be quick. He pushed his way to the shop's door and nearly lost the bag, with his purchases, to the man opening the door and shoving his way in.

¡Maldito sea! These tourists were annoying at the best of times, but this one – he seemed to be following him!

Greg watched Roberto stride away, then, putting on his most disarming smile, he walked into the book shop and joined the chatty customers.

Chapter 17 – Pamela's Thursday Morning

Miguel stopped by, unfashionably early, and whisked Granny Em away for another day out in his ancient Mercedes. Pamela was a little worried as the view from her studio window showed him pulling out, into the steady stream of cars heading down the hill for the local market, with no warning but a great deal of pressing his horn. There was a loud screeching of brakes and she could hear her mother-in-law shrieking instructions and describing hazards, on the road, in the street and on the pavement as the car alternately jerked and braked its screeching way towards the harbour.

Once the road noise went back to normal, Pamela headed out of the apartment and down the stairs.

It wasn't long before she was having a great deal of fun, glad of an excuse to rummage through the storeroom in the basement. She was pleased that she'd thought to rent it, just before Sally moved in. With Raoul's help, it was filled with all the memorabilia and papers, bits and bobs that had filled her married life, but now felt too sad to look at every day.

Anyway, Sally needed space for her belongings and it wouldn't have been good for her to be reminded constantly of her father.

The basement room was small and windowless, so it had not added much to the rent. There were no sockets to plug in a light, just a single bare lightbulb that dangled with glum determination from the middle of the ceiling – its persistence not matched by the feeble light it cast over the room. Pamela, however, was armed with a felt-tip pen, two carrier bags and a storm lamp. Everyone in town had at least one storm lamp. The electricity company did its best, but the severity of winter storms and the deluge of rain that came with the *Gota Fria*, each year, meant that even their best efforts were frequently beaten by Nature's unpredictable Mediterranean extremes.

She'd left a note, stuck to the outside of the flat's front door, to say where she was, in case Sally got home before she finished, or Raoul needed her. She was secretly hoping that one of them would see it and pop down. Coming down the narrow steps to the basement hadn't been difficult, with little to carry, but returning with a bag full of treasures might be a bit more than she could manage, without help.

It was easy to forget that she'd been so ill and to think herself fitter and stronger than she was, especially now that she was recovering, but on days like today, she remembered.

As most of the boxes had been brought down by Raoul, in his odd moments of free time, and piled in haste, there was no rhyme nor reason to where anything was placed.

She'd been too distraught, then, to label any of the boxes as they were packed away – a big mistake she decided now, as she ruefully gazed around the room.

She took a deep breath and started systematically,

on the largest of the boxes. Once eliminated, each box was pushed out of the way. She was able to use the first two finished, one on top of the other, as a makeshift seat, which helped.

Making sure that she labelled each box with a summary of the contents, she worked steadily round the room dragging the finished boxes aside. None were very heavy, the boxes with books and records had gone to a local retreat for the terminally ill.

Most of those left held clothes and shoes, holiday mementoes and things that she ought to send to charity one day, but not now, another time.

...She loved that shirt.

...She remembered finding that tie on a trip to Madrid.

...Maybe she could wear that sweater at home when it got colder.

She was so far into her stride, by the time she found the boxes from the office, that she almost forgot she was looking for the phone, the camera and their memory sticks. She was just about to return the bag of camera gear to the box she'd taken it from, when she realised what she was doing and knew she could stop now.

It was just as well. She had to get back up the stairs and she couldn't risk getting tired.

She didn't need to go through any of the other boxes, this trip. She sat for a while, nursing the phone that had been stored with the camera, remembering the day she'd bought it for him and his sheer enjoyment, using it, playing with it, fiddling with it, until, a few weeks later, news from the doctor had wiped the joy from both of their lives.

She removed the memory chips, popped them into her pocket and put the empty phone back into the box. The camera might as well go upstairs, in the bag, she doubted there was much on it, in the way of photos but, now it was emptied, Sally might want to charge it and use it for her blog. Tidying up the last bits and pieces of what was left in the box only took a couple of minutes and the room looked much better now, even in this state.

Not to worry, she thought, looking around the half-organised room, *I am not afraid anymore, I can embrace this now, own it, sort it. I'll be back soon room, very soon. At least you no longer resemble an episode of 'Storage Wars'.*

Sighing deeply, she put her remaining finds, with the camera, pen and lamp in the bag, switched off the light and locked the door behind her. She didn't look farther down the corridor into the basement shadows, so she'd no idea that she wasn't alone as she turned towards the stairs. She'd barely struggled up more than the first step, when she felt the blow. When she fell forward it was as if the stairs tilted up towards her. Losing hold of the bag, her hands automatically flew up to brace her fall.

Dizzy with fear and pain, she felt the bag being moved from where it had fallen against her leg. She was also aware of being pulled and pushed about as whoever it was shifted her off the stairs, to free the exit. She was left lying on her side facing the wall, so saw nothing of her attacker. She did, however, hear the attacker grunting and panting with effort as they hurried up the stairs, slamming doors behind them as they fled the building.

Always Right

Bruised and frightened, Pamela lay there, as still as she could, mentally checking herself and trying to decide what hurt most, the loss of her feeling of sanctuary and safety in this part of her home, or her head, which throbbed.

Sally would come soon; she would know what to do. Just now, Pamela didn't feel like being the grown-up. For the first time since Sally had arrived to live in Spain, as much as she enjoyed her company, she finally accepted that she did really need her daughter. What's more, she needed her now.

Drifting in and out of consciousness, Pamela couldn't be sure how much time had passed before she heard Sally's voice at the top of the stairs. She was, however, awake enough to register, with faint surprise, that the police appeared to be there, already. How could they possible have known?

Earlier, Sally had only needed to wait at the restaurant for about forty minutes before Pedro joined them and signalled to the sergeant that the last member of the Forensic Team had gone. The back yard had been locked and sealed, the rest of the restaurant had been returned to Mario, who looked surprisingly happy for a man who'd spent most of the day being questioned by the police.

Pedro was dying to tell Sally what the owner of Café Mediterraneo had told Sofía about Marianne, but he couldn't, at least not while the sergeant was still with them.

Sofía was on the telephone arranging to meet Roberto at Lola's café at five pm, giving them an hour before Lola had to open for the evening trade. They waited, in silence, for her to finish. After her call, they were free to walk Sally back to her apartment and see what Pamela had found. Sofía kept the conversation light, telling Sally about her last visit to the Port, before this.

The Guardia had been called in to investigate what was thought might be a smuggling ring, bringing in heavy drugs. She'd arrived on the scene just after the National Police (who were taking the lead) had burst in through the front doors of a villa near the harbour.

Inside, they'd discovered a little old man, in his early nineties. He'd been bulk-buying Viagra on the internet and then distributing it through a couple of local bars known for their older clientele. His wife, the only other member of the 'gang', had been baking Cannabis cakes for a list of elderly locals who suffered from various conditions, from rheumatism to mild dementia, all were taking it hoping it would reduce their symptoms.

What had delighted Sofía was that the drug dealing couple had put age restrictions on the customers they would take for both their products. They refused to let the drugs go to anyone under seventy.

Their defence was that they didn't sell drugs, they distributed them; they were presents. The prosecutor, however, had proof that they'd accepted gifts in exchange and as far as he was concerned there was no legal distinction between bartering for something you wanted and selling. The couple had been arrested and convicted. The judge had no choice. Growing a few plants for personal consumption was

AtWays Right

one thing, but this was much more like the start of a small farm.

Walking into the Correos Square, from the side opposite to the apartment, they were startled to see someone, dressed in black, tearing out of the main entrance to Sally's building. Whoever it was, he or she was moving too fast and was too far away to see clearly, but the runner looked furtive. Running out of a building and away from the police, didn't look good.

Pedro yelled in Spanish into his lapel microphone and sprinted after the fleeing shape.

Sally automatically looked up to her and Pamela's balcony, but it looked empty.

The flat was dark and silent.

She and Sofía ran into the building, through the doorway the visitor had left wide open, and raced up the stairs to the apartment, knocking on Raoul's door as they passed.

Pamela's apartment door was locked and everything looked secure. Sally unlocked it and they both moved quickly through the flat, meeting again at the entrance not having seen any sign of Pamela.

As they walked back onto the landing, Sofía noticed a sticky notelet half under the door, where it must have fallen. The handwriting looked indecipherable.

"Wait Sally, can you read this? Is this your mother's writing?"

"Yes, it says, 'In basement, come down, I expect I will have found something useful for the police by the time you see this. In any event, whatever it is, I may need a hand carrying the bag upstairs, please'.

It was timed three hours ago. Do you suppose she's still downstairs?" Leaving Sally's keys in the door, they abandoned the flat and dashed down the stairs to the basement. A rather surprised Raoul, who'd finally answered the knocking, followed, a little more slowly and very puzzled, having first taken the time to lock both apartment doors.

He brought both sets of keys with him.

When they found Pamela at the bottom of the stairs she was drifting in and out of consciousness.

Raoul called for the ambulance and Sofía called the forensics team back to work.

Sally just sat on the floor and held her mother's hand, talking to her calmly, reassuringly, about what was happening and what would happen next.

The ambulance was very fast to arrive, as the Salud, where the ambulances waited outside the Accident and Emergency Unit, was barely 300 metres from the apartment.

With the paramedics came Pedro, who'd not been able to catch up with the intruder. By the time Pedro had run behind the restaurant, whoever it was had jumped onto a motor bike and roared off up the street, before he was able to read the number plate. After radioing in a description of the bike and its rider. Pedro made his way back to the apartment. With his help, the two medics managed to get Pamela onto a stretcher and into the ambulance. Sally tried to get into the ambulance with her and was astonished when her way was barred.

"No Sally, let them go, they will be more able to treat Pamela in the ambulance, while they travel, if you are not in the way." Pedro held her shoulders and looked deep into her eyes until she nodded and stopped resisting. "I'll ask the sergeant if I can take you to the hospital, she'll want Pamela to make a statement and I think it's important that we hear her story as soon as she comes round."

Greg was very angry. He'd been seen by Pedro and might have been identified by Sally and made to look guilty, just because he'd been leaving the building when they arrived. He didn't like being chased, especially by the bitch's lap dog; plus, he had nothing to do with whatever sick game the café-owner's boyfriend was playing at.

He'd only gone into the building to see what Sally's apartment was like and what the old woman was up to – talk about bad timing! The woman must have been in the basement while he was upstairs, looking round. Now his hired motorbike had been seen and they might have got the registration. He didn't need this crap! He so did not need it! Now they would waste time looking for him instead of the people behind the killings. He needed this killing spree to be over, he had his own agenda to sort out and this mess was getting in the way.

Now, he would have to file a report with the rental company and tell them the bike had been stolen, then he'd get rid of the bike and find another way of moving around. He needed to find something off the books – everything here seemed to involve passports, ID and paperwork. Hired vehicles were too easily traceable. Maybe he should go back to the hotel and look at the options …once the bike was in a ditch.

Chapter 18 – Thursday Afternoon

It was clear to Sofía that Pedro was going with Sally whether he had permission or not, so it was best he had it. His obvious concern for Sally was going to be too distracting to make it worth having him around, here, anyway, so she was quick to give her permission.

Before Sally left, however, she asked her for permission to look around the flat again, as Raoul had the keys and could supervise.

Sally barely heard her and just nodded, agreeing to whatever Sofía said. By the time Raoul and Sofía had turned to re-enter the building, she was already yards away, running down the side street where Pedro had told her he'd left his car.

Pedro raced after her and, panting heavily, managed to press the unlock button on his key and climb in the driver's side in time for her to yank open his passenger door and jump in. "It will be OK, *Cariña*, it will be OK – just strap in."

His voice was soothing – but the look on his face was determined, so she leaned back in the seat and closed her eyes. She trusted him, she needed his strength, but she still repeated the mantra in her head that she'd started when she saw her mother lying still at the bottom of the steps. *Be alright, be alright, be alright!*

Even with the clear road, thanks to the car's siren *whup, whupping* as Pedro accelerated down the main road to the Regional Hospital, the ambulance still beat them to the entrance of Accident and Emergency. By the time they arrived, Pamela had been admitted and was, "Receiving medical attention."

The attendant on reception was no more informative, although Pedro did confirm that there was a police guard outside her room. Once the receptionist had given them a numbered ticket, Pedro steered Sally to the soulless, moulded wooden seats that lined the A and E waiting area where an enterprising soul, at some point, had painted a mural of cute cartoon animals from a popular children's film. Sally vaguely recognised them, but her mind was like wool. When Pedro took the next seat to her, she leaned her head into his proffered shoulder and felt the warmth of his arm around her. For the first time since the shock of finding her mother, she felt safe, protected.

They stayed that way, silent, together, until a young nurse came to the opening of the waiting room and called Sally's name. It had been two hours since they arrived, Sally could barely walk to the nurse. Pedro took her elbow and stayed beside her as they went down the long corridor. All that Sally could think about was that she had taken the same walk, the day her father died.

The machine beeping next to her mother's silent, prostrate form was frightening, until Pamela opened her eyes, saw her daughter and smiled.

Sally's knees started to give way, again. Pedro

only just managed to get her to a seat, in time.

"I am alright, child, stop fretting, you're stuck with me for a while longer yet! My head is sore and, because I was a bit woozy, they are keeping me in for observation, tonight. I expect I'll be able to come home tomorrow morning. Hello Pedro, thank you for being there for Sally. I am so sorry. I messed up, didn't I? The camera is gone, they took it along with my favourite jumper of your father's." Pamela looked surprisingly cheerful.

"Pedro, is the skirt I was wearing in that cupboard? Please." He stood up and, delving into the small cupboard to the side of her bed, got the skirt out, showing it to Pamela. "Yes, good, there's a deep pocket on the right-hand side. Be a dear will you, please, and see if the chips are still in there."

Astonished, Pedro and Sally stared at the memory chips he'd just pulled from Pamela's skirt pocket. "Yes," she said, "they are the ones – I pulled them out of the phone and the camera before I closed up. The phone I left in the storeroom. Shame about the camera though, I thought you could use it, Sally."

They told her what they'd seen and what had alerted them to something being wrong and about the chase and the motorbike.

Pamela then went through everything she could remember, regretful that she didn't really see anything. She was able to tell Pedro about the wheezing on the stairs, though, "It was very distinctive, raspy, like your gran was, Sally, before she went on to an asthma nebuliser. I also think I heard the *click-hissy* sound of an inhaler being pressed, when whoever it was got to the top step.

They must have stayed in the building for at least ten minutes for you to have seen them leaving. Maybe they needed to rest for a minute or two, but I am surprised whoever it was could outrun you, Pedro, although the length of the square is a big head start. They must have left the bike very near the Pizza Restaurant's loading bay. Maybe one of the staff saw it."

Sally stayed with her mother, while Pedro rang the First Sergeant to update her, then went to fetch his laptop from the car. When he returned, he uploaded each chip's contents onto his laptop and, when done, opened the image viewer so that the three of them could see the screen.

Most of the photos were like the ones Sally and Pedro had already seen... one, however, was very interesting.

Egnacio, his son, Marianne and Frau Schmeckler were all looking very interested in something being shown to them by the woman at whose stall Egnacio had been photographed earlier.

Something that glittered.

Taking a moment to get Pamela's Health number off her SIP card, Pedro used her code to access the free patient wi-fi and emailed the photo to Sofía – marking it urgent.

Sofía had taken a thorough look around Pamela's studio, while Raoul checked that the apartment was secure. She took this unexpected opportunity to take close-ups of the dress and the painting with her smartphone. It had a higher resolution than Pedro's less expensive model and did macro shots very well.

She was fascinated by the detail and the level of accuracy that Pamela had achieved in paint. Pamela's eye almost seemed to have caught something on the canvas that the dress itself appeared designed to disguise. How intriguing.

While her phone was handy, Sofía tried a quick search for seamstresses in Puerto Amarillo, to see if anything could point to the contact details of the Madrid tailoress who'd made the dress. Angelica was at the top, and in fact filled the first few pages – there was nothing about any new tailoress, dress designer, dressmaker or seamstress moving into the port.

Oh well, no matter – the parents of the young girl in the painting would know who they'd commissioned to make it, and it was time they were interviewed.

Raoul finished his check at around the same time Sofía was ready to leave the apartment. He locked the flat door and offered her a coffee but, tempted though she was, she had too much to do, so they parted outside Raoul's apartment. Raoul promised to keep an eye open for Sally's gran and to make sure she was alright, and Sofía made her way down to the basement to see if forensics had any news to help her.

By the time Pedro rang to let her know that Pamela looked as if she was going to be OK, Sofía had signed off the forensic team from the basement steps and the area around the storeroom and was making her way to the interview with Lola.

She'd almost arrived at the café when her phone beeped. It was an email from Pedro marked urgent.

She opened the attachment and stared at it in dismay.

Normally, the family of a murder victim was put under close scrutiny, as a preliminary to the first part of the investigation. Sofía cursed to herself. Looking at the photo that had just popped up on her phone, maybe she'd made a massive mistake. Still, it was six years ago. Could these old photos really still be important? How did the person who attacked Pamela know anything about them? How did they know that Pamela was looking for them? There were more questions than answers and, if she didn't answer some soon, she would lose the case to an inspector. First, however, Lola and Roberto were waiting for her.

Maybe they could put a name to the unidentified woman who kept cropping up.

Chapter 19 – Granny Em's Afternoon

Granny Em was delighted to be spending time with Miguel, she had always liked him and his wife. It was a shock how much older he was now, compared to when she and Frank had lived in the Puerto all those years ago.

Losing Marta had aged him, just like Frank dying had added years to her.

It had been a struggle for her to leave Spain and go back to the UK, but with both her husband and her son gone, it had felt right. She'd forgotten how the sun's warmth made her feel years younger and how much she'd missed the soft creamy yellow stone of the walls and church that had given the port its name.

It was lovely to be visiting old favourite places with someone who shared memories of those happy times. He might be older, but he was certainly just as dashing as always.

She'd felt guilty leaving Pamela to cope alone in Spain, all those years ago, but Pamela had a life here. With a sick, then terminally ill husband, Pamela had forged a career to sustain them both. By the time she was widowed, she had a long list of clients, was earning enough to be comfortable and had a strong local network of friends.

Emma, with income of her own, her son and husband gone, and not wanting to be a nuisance to Pamela, had needed to find a new life in the UK near her remaining daughter and grandchildren.

Her main reason for visiting, after all this time, was to check on Sally. She missed the regular visits Sally had made to her from the various places she'd lived in England. She had met Sally's fiancé, Greg, and had found him thoroughly unnerving. He was incredibly narcissistic and seemed to see the whole world as only being there to make him happy, make him look good and serve his needs. She was hugely relieved when Sally had seen the light and ditched the swine. Pamela was lucky to have never met him.

Seeing Sally so bubbly, interacting with her mother and their neighbours was a relief. It was obvious that Sally was happy, so that was one less worry.

It was a beautiful day and Miguel was good company. It was time for her to start thinking about her own future, after all, it was never too late to grasp a little happiness. It might be nice to spend a few days up in the mountains and enjoy good company, fine wine, warm days and cool evenings.

She sent a short text to Sally, to tell her not to expect her home until Monday and then, after switching off her phone, turned her concentration to enjoying her sudden freedom from worry and her fascinating and handsome companion.

Chapter 20 – Frau Schmeckler's Afternoon

Frau Schmeckler was tired and more than a little fed up with how Herbert, meant to make her life easier, had thrown such a huge spanner in the works. She could see it shortening her stay in Spain, rapidly. She hadn't believed it was Herbert and Fritz in Egnacio's, until the girls had reported back to her. Who could have believed he was the thief?

Clearly, Egnacio had just seen it as another earning opportunity. He'd certainly been delighted to let her know that it was back in his possession.

Much good it had done him.

Unbelievable!

She'd definitely made a mistake letting their other partner take Marianne down to see who collected the damned thing.

Marianne had rung, shortly after arriving at the shop to confirm that Egnacio still had the brooch. having gone in on her own and found him there, dead. Her first panicked thought was to phone for advice.

She'd been extremely clear. Under no circumstances should Marianne alert the police – she should go back to their partner, waiting in the nearest café, and wait to see who came in to get the brooch, just like they had planned.

Telling Marianne to get the brooch out of the drawer and leave it on the counter was a stroke of genius, as it would draw the thief into the shop. Then they could see who it was and follow them, to find out where the thief figured in their current dilemma.

The two women had messed up completely. It had been a few minutes before they'd been able to extricate themselves from the café and, although they'd seen him run up the street past the Charity shop, they'd lost him somewhere near there.

Marianne had walked back to the book shop and positioned herself in the window where she could see both up and down the street. Her colleague having other work to do had left her to it. Eventually, Marianne had bought a heap of random books from a bin, to explain her lengthy stay in the shop and walked up to the first junction. Passing the restaurant, on the way, she'd seen a notice on the door, asking for a bookkeeper.

As she'd explained, later, when all three women met for an update, it made more sense than wandering up and down the street, every day, with a bag of books. She could work for the restaurant doing their accounts for a few days, without raising any suspicion.

It would be a perfect place from which to watch out for Herbert, discover what he was up to and find out who he was working for.

Marianne had never had the chance to report back.

So, what Frau Schmeckler needed to do now was work out who was moving in on her operation and who was killing her business partners.

She needed to work it out fast, too, just in case she was nearing the top of the list.

Lola hadn't been sure if she was happy about the increase in her business thanks to the café's proximity to a murder scene. However, she noticed it starting to go back to normal, soon after the Café Mediterraneo reopened, and was sad about that, too. At least she'd been forewarned by Roberto, so it hadn't been as much of a blow as it would have been otherwise.

Many of the more prurient, newly acquired customers were already flocking to eat *inside* a murder scene, rather than *near* one, but, thanks to Roberto's warning, she'd made sure that, before they left her, all had vouchers in their pockets for a free glass of wine with their next meal at Lola's, so maybe some would be back...

She was glad that Roberto was going to sit in on the Sergeant's interview, so put a couple of her better bottles of wine in the fridge, to chill. A mellow mood wouldn't hurt the Guardia, whoever they sent, and might help her relax enough to recall whatever they wanted to know.

She went back over everything she could remember, not just about Monday, but also about the weeks before.

Angelica had been ecstatic that the flat spanning the top floor of the building she shared with Egnacio's shop had been let. Even more so, when she discovered that it was let to a seamstress from Madrid, who specialised in making exotic costumes for fiestas and debutante processions.

She'd shown Lola the woman's website and it had been very impressive, with beautifully worked dresses for women and girls, amazing matador style suits for men. To produce the exquisitely embroidered and exotic costumes for the fiestas, she imported materials from all over the world and she was coming to Puerto Amarillo; who would have thought?

Angelica was sweet, she didn't see it as competition, even when her best customer had ordered the Reina dress from the new woman. "It doesn't matter Lola," Angelica told her. "The woman does all her own work, and takes a month, at least, to produce one outfit of the quality that they will order. In that time, I and my ladies will have made most of the less complicated dresses for the rest of the ladies in waiting. Even though they're not as expensive and, even though I have to pay my ladies, I'll be far better off this year than most years, when I had to take the work-intensive 'prestigious' orders or lose face. She can charge high prices to make it worthwhile for her – I've never been able to command such fees. It's brilliant that she'll be in our building too, as we may get spin-off orders through her, or from clients she has to turn away through being busy."

Angelica was full of news, every day, before the Madrid woman arrived, about the expensive furniture and state-of-the-art sewing equipment that was going up the back stairs to the new flat.

However, it all went quiet after she arrived. Angelica had yet even to meet the woman, although her own increased dress orders had more than matched her predictions.

From what he'd said, Egnacio had seemed indifferent to the woman, as long as it didn't interfere with his business. "Maybe her clients will buy nice jewellery for the girls to wear; maybe they won't ...who can tell?" he'd muttered to Lola, over a rare coffee, not long after the woman moved in.

Egnacio never said much about anything, besides the tourists, but then everyone she knew always had something to say about the tourists. Getting him to say anything about the seamstress from Madrid had been an effort, but she was curious, the woman was keeping a very low profile. Thinking about it, even now, Lola still had no idea what she looked like.

Lola's brother, José, was more popular than ever with his school friends now he'd been involved in a real murder. He'd even had a group of kids trailing round after him asking for autographs.

Since he was fifteen and old enough to know that this fame would be short-lived, he was going to enjoy it as much as he could.

Just for once, it helped that his sister's boyfriend was in the Policía Local. Normally, it might have made him unpopular that he had a policeman, nearly in the family. Still, Roberto was a nice enough bloke, a bit short-tempered, but he was usually fair, so it had not affected José's standing. His part in the murderer's escape had made him a local celebrity, especially when he'd embellished it a little, to make it appear that the collision was a deliberate *ploy*, trying to stop a jewel thief and murderer!

He'd even got a date, after revealing to Alicia that

he was being interviewed by the police later, so, if she would like to meet him in the café for supper, it would need to be after the police interview rather than before. Hook, line and sinker, he thought as he arranged the time.

When First Sergeant Gonzales finally interviewed him, however, he'd added little to his first account of the accident. He was able to confirm that it was Herbert he'd seen, and that Herbert had something blue in his hand. Having seen the photo, he also agreed that he might have seen him around the Port before, near the bars, but not with the dog.

Not that he went into bars, of course.

Lola was surprised when the sergeant arrived before Roberto.

She collected one of the bottles, which she'd chilled earlier, along with a corkscrew and three glasses, setting them up on the table before she sat. The sergeant accepted the wine, appreciatively, it had been a long day.

They sat in companionable silence; Roberto had already texted both that he was on his way.

The text to the sergeant was a little longer, though.

The motorbike had been identified as stolen from the road behind Egnacio and Lola's premises about two hours before the attack. Roberto would be late, as he was stopping by the station, with his tablet, to get all the photos from Pedro's emails, Pamela's computer and the new ones from the chip just sent.

Sofía was pleased, it would make it easier to show Lola the photos that might trigger a memory.

Eventually, it was Lola who broke the silence and asked the first question. "Is there any more news about Sally's mum?"

Sofía was startled – the speed that news travelled round the port was staggering, although Lola was Roberto's girlfriend. Still, it had been indiscreet of him if he were the source.

Lola saw the expression of dismay on Sofía's face and guessed the cause, "No, it was not Roberto, he never tells me police business, ever. José told me. He was in the square delivering a message for Angelica, when the thief came out, before the ambulance came. He told me all about it, when he came back. She walked right past him, apparently."

"What? He saw him... her... close to? Did he recognise her? Where is he, we need to talk to him?"

"José is in the kitchen, having a snack before he goes off to choir, I'll get him." Lola was only gone a few minutes, but Roberto had arrived by the time she returned with José.

José's news came first.

"I was walking out of the restaurant, underneath Pamela and Sally's flat and this woman came panting past. She came out of Sally's building and was carrying a bag. She looked very flustered and kept looking round, like she didn't want to be seen, which made me look right at her, of course. She was dressed in black and looked a bit old for all that running. She was making a shocking amount of noise as she ran, so I stopped walking to make sure she was OK. I thought, at first, that she might be Sally's Gran, I knew she was staying, but when I looked at her properly, she didn't look like a foreigner. I was just about to call out, when she disappeared around the corner of the café. I turned away to get the message I was delivering, out of my rucksack and, a few minutes later, a man ran past and jumped on the motorbike that was parked behind the bins. Switching on the engine, he kicked off the stand and drove off really fast. Pedro ran all the way across the square in the time it took the man to get from the corner to the bike, if he hadn't been so quick starting and roaring off, Pedro would have caught him. Quite impressive for a policeman. I'm never running away from Pedro, unless I'm on a bike, he is fast."

José was obviously torn between disappointment that whoever it was had got away, and admiration for his bike handling. "I don't know why Pedro was chasing the man though, it was the old woman who looked guilty, the man just looked annoyed. She'd gone into an alleyway out of sight by the time Pedro turned back from losing the biker. She wasn't the one who hurt Pamela though, was she?"

Sofía looked sternly at him and said, "There's a very good chance that she was, José, have you seen her before?"

"Oh." José sounded thoroughly deflated "No, I don't think so. I thought I recognised the bike though, if you want to find him. Maybe he was acting as a distraction, so she could get away, she was a bit slow to try and outrun Pedro. I have seen a bike like it on Calle Rosas, behind us, here. I would recognise the biker again and the woman – or at least her eyes; I think, they were blue, but she was definitely Spanish, I could hear her muttering swear words between pants and nobody can swear as well as a Spaniard!" He thought for a bit, "Yes, I would recognise her if I saw her again, if that helps. I'll definitely keep my eyes open though, when I do my deliveries."

"Do not challenge either of them, José, if you see them again, use your mobile and text or ring me, your sister, Pedro or Roberto. Here, key in Pedro's number and mine, now, I'm sure you have your sister's and Roberto's." Sofía was calm but clear. She didn't want to alarm either José or his sister, but, if José had been seen by the attacker, he might be at risk. "Do not tell anyone else about seeing the man *or* the woman, not your friends, your girlfriend, no one, do you understand, José. It will help us to catch them, if they think that *nobody* saw them."

José agreed, quietly hoping that he would have time to stop the only person he *had* told from spreading the news.

"Before you go back inside, José, I would like to show you and your sister some pictures taken at an exhibition you both went to six years ago. It would be a great help, if you could name any of the people you recognise. Mainly so that we can eliminate most of them from the current enquiry. You are a bit young to remember them from the Exhibition, José, but you may have seen some of them since." Sofía signalled to Roberto to open his tablet and he took out his pen and pad making a show of taking notes of the names that were offered, as she scrolled slowly through the photos.

There were few surprises. The representatives from local shops were familiar to most of the people at the table. Egnacio and his son were, of course, known to them both. José and Lola immediately identified Marianne as one of the women sitting in the restaurant, when José crashed his bike. Neither knew Frau Schmeckler or the woman who was showing the others something shiny and who'd talked to Egnacio from her dress stand, although both agreed that she might have been the other witness at the table. However, Lola did suggest that, if it was important, they might want to nip in to see Angelica. She would recognise anyone in the business of making Fiesta and presentation dresses or anything related. Angelica would be at work for at least another hour and she was only next door.

After José had gone back into the kitchen, to grab his bag, before cycling off for his date, Sofía took Lola through everything she could remember from that day, a couple more times until, satisfied, she rose and asked Roberto to spare her a few moments with Angelica – after which they would call it a day.

Lola was delighted and promised Roberto his favourite supper, as he was finishing early enough to enjoy it with her before the evening rush. She did invite Sofía, as an afterthought, but the sergeant grinned and said that her meal would be waiting at home – thanks all the same!

Angelica was quite mystified when they called in to see her. She'd never been involved in police business before, but wasn't it shocking about Egnacio?

She rattled on for a few minutes, before they were able to calm her down long enough to view the photos. They then went through them slowly, as they had with Lola, with Roberto making a big show of

133

making taking notes again.

When they got to the costume exhibition, however, they were astonished when Angelica started to tell them the names of the stall holders, even when there were no people in the photos. "Oh, well... it is my business you know. I go to every exhibition, I was probably at that one, on a different day, I have to know what the styles and fashions will be from the big dealers or I can't compete."

However, when they got to the mystery woman, talking to Marianne and Egnacio, even though it was clear, they were disappointed to discover nothing ...she didn't know her.

The next photo showed the same woman talking to Egnacio, but with him partially hidden behind a black dress that was hanging in front of the stall. Roberto was flicking through the pictures faster than Sofía would have liked and had already flicked to the next shot, but Angelica asked if she could go back one, so she could take another look at it.

"I don't know the person sitting there, but I know that dress, it was a traditional Spanish widow's, straight out of a 19th century fashion plate, it made quite a stir when it was exhibited, because the styles that year were mainly bright primary colours. This dress, however, was stunning, elegant, timeless. It was designed and made by my new neighbour, the *mujer de Madrid*. Look, I can show you her website, she has some shots of it in her portfolio."

Chapter 21 – Raoul's Friday Morning

It was obvious to Raoul, when Pamela phoned him, that she was delighted to be allowed home. She asked him if he would be kind enough to come and get her and to bring Sally with him, plus a change of clothes for her.

Raoul tried ringing Sally, before knocking on the apartment door, but she didn't answer her mobile. She did, however, respond to the hammering on the door, looking remarkably sparkly and happy, as did Pedro, who was just leaving the shower with little more than a towel round him as Raoul stepped into the flat. "Oh! Mmm! I see! Shall I go?" Raoul spluttered, taken aback!

"Don't be silly, Raoul!" Sally smiled "We had the locksmith in last night, as the keys were missing and Pedro insisted on staying the night, sleeping on the couch! Look, he brought his own bodyguard too!" Cha-Cha loped out from behind the settee and planted her front paws on Raoul's shoulders, trying to lick any breakfast he might inadvertently have splashed on his nose, cheeks and forehead. "Get down Cha-Cha, you know Raoul is far too fastidious to have food on his face" She laughed at the dog and pulled him off Raoul. Raoul was totally astounded; he'd known Cha-Cha from a puppy and never managed to get the dog to do anything. Here was Sally, a friend of barely a few hours, and she was ordering the dog around as if she was her own pet!

Pedro's first job that morning was to meet the sergeant at the home of Dolores Garcia, Pamela's young sitter, to make enquires about the seamstress. He was pretty sure now, after an update from Sofía over the phone that morning, that they knew who and where the Madrid designer was, but there were other questions about the dress that they wanted to ask, and they needed to be sure.

He promised Sally that, while he was there, he would make sure that Dolores and her family knew about the attack on Pamela and that she needed to postpone their sitting arrangement for a few days, while she rested.

Sally gave Pedro the 'spare' set of new keys left by the locksmith, so he could secure the apartment, when he left. He promised to put them in their locked mailbox, when he let himself out.

Within minutes, she and Raoul were on their way to the car. They might have been even quicker, but Raoul had to endure a long list of instructions from Pedro about keeping Sally and Pamela safe.

As they drove to the hospital, he was glad of the opportunity to tell Sally all that Pedro had told him about Carlos and his activities in the Square. "I cannot understand it, Sally, he comes home, he tells me that everything is good between us, that he loves me – then Pedro tells me that Carlos is getting out of a minibus and sneaking round to a travel agent." Raoul was visibly distraught and the car, clearly sensing his mood, swung from one lane to another on each corner.

"Raoul, I know you're upset, but killing us both is not on today's agenda. Anyway, you know this will be a storm in a teacup!" Sally stopped, seeing the confusion on Raoul's face, his English was so good, she often forgot it was not his first language. "I mean," she continued, "it will turn out to be something that was never meant to hurt you, Raoul, I am sure he loves you, unreservedly. I have always been a little jealous of you guys, you are so good together."

"Do you really think so? You don't think that there is someone else?"

Crossing her fingers that she was right, she replied, "Never! He would be mad to risk losing you. If you were otherwise inclined, I would have snapped you straight up!" Pacified, Raoul parked the car in the Hospital's underground car park, and they made their way to the Observation Ward.

Pamela was relieved to hear that Granny Em was off on an adventure and had missed all the excitement. "Her heart isn't that good, you know, Sally, she would have just fretted and exhausted everyone. Much better if we can tell her all about it when she gets back. Maybe we'll know who is behind all this, by then." Pamela was ready to leave and couldn't wait to take the fresh clothes from Sally, so that she could change. Raoul opened the cupboard next to the bed and took out the clothes she'd worn when attacked. Together they straightened everything and folded the clothes, placing them tidily into the bag.

Sally checked the cupboard to make sure it was

empty and noticed something shiny – at the back. She reached in and pulled it out. It was a long thin sliver of cellophane – like the shredded plastic stuff that she'd seen as padding in packages. How odd, she thought, looking round for a wastepaper basket. Not seeing one, she popped it into the bag, she could throw it into the bin later.

On the way home, Pamela regaled them with small anecdotes of her short hospital stay. "Seriously, there were clowns wandering up and down the corridor. I have seen them in the Chemo room, before, singing 'jolly' songs, but I expect that is a place with lots of people who would like to be cheered up. I've never seen them wandering about near intensive care before, it was a bit of a surprise. The nurse said that they are volunteers and they like to visit the waiting areas near intensive, to try and cheer the families waiting for news. I said the children must love it and she just looked surprised and said no, the clowns are for the grown-ups! It was all very well-meaning, but a bit unnerving!"

Even Raoul looked surprised, answering "I hope none of us ever have to come here again to find out! How are you really? Would you like to have lunch before we get home, or shall I take you straight there?"

"I would like to eat, but I would like to go home too. Join us Raoul and we'll send downstairs to the restaurant for lunch. You two can share the wine, while you tell me everything you know about what happened to me. Have my keys turned up at the station yet? A nurse said that one of the ambulance men was going to hand them in at the police station on their way back to the Salud. Apparently, they fell out of my hands after I was moved, and he found them on the ambulance floor. He asked her to tell me, so I didn't worry. More importantly, the person who hit me, have they been caught yet?" Sally promised to ask for the keys at the police station, later. Then, between them Sally and Raoul brought Pamela up to speed. By the time they reached home, organised food and settled in over a bottle of wine, the news had also included Raoul's latest Carlos update. "I agree with Sally, Carlos and you are too perfect together, Raoul, there has to be a simple explanation," was Pamela's initial reaction. "Have you asked him?"

Raoul looked at her, open-mouthed, "You mean ask him, out loud, face to face?"

"Yes!" She gave him her stern look "What is the absolute worst that can happen? It cannot be as corrosive as all this worrying!" Raoul looked very unsure, but, when Sally agreed with her mother, he eventually agreed that he would tackle Carlos when he came home.

Satisfied, they let the conversation gradually move back to the two murders and the attack. That topic was soon exhausted, as none of them had received an update from Pedro all day, so Raoul told them of Sofía's admiration of Pamela's portrait and how interested she was in the dress and its maker.

"Sofía – sorry – First Sergeant Gonzales, has children, hasn't she? Maybe she wants a portrait," murmured Pamela thoughtfully. Raoul and Sally exchanged glances, but neither expressed their doubt. Pamela caught the look, though, and started to wonder.

Chapter 22 – Roberto's Friday Morning

Seeing Pedro dashing across the square, in the early hours of Friday morning, astonished Roberto. Pedro must have just left the English girl's apartment building; he'd thought her to be a much slower worker than that. Still, dark waters – maybe she would be someone worth developing if he had to stay here much longer. Lola was getting boringly clingy.

It was as well that he'd decided to finish his coffee, before going up to Pamela's apartment again. If he'd gone up as soon as Raoul and Sally left for the hospital, he thought wryly, that might have resulted in a difficult conversation. Explaining to Pedro why he possessed Pamela's keys, might have been awkward, too. The dratted man seemed to be everywhere.

Roberto had been angry when his carefully laid plan was stymied by the Inspector choosing Pedro over him to work with the Guardia. Worse, he'd lost his beat to a new recruit and had to take over Pedro's patch – although Lola was an unexpected bonus!

Still, the advantage of taking over Pedro's desk duties meant he'd been on reception, yesterday, when Pamela was rushed to hospital. He was just finishing his shift, when Pamela's ambulance man dropped into the police station.

Roberto couldn't believe his luck, first, he had all the photos that the Guardia were researching on his tablet and now the paramedic had just handed him the Wright woman's keys, at the moment he was about to leave the desk. Talk about timing! Making a great show of logging the keys in, without actually doing it, he'd thanked the man. Then, once the paramedic had gone, he slipped the keys into his pocket and left the station.

He'd arrived at the square as Sofía was leaving, so he waited out of sight until she was gone. Minutes later, having retrieved the bag from his car, he let himself into Pamela and Sally's flat.

Mother would not have been pleased had he come away empty-handed this time. Not after all the trouble she'd gone to. Not happy at all ...but he couldn't. He couldn't and he hadn't. He'd done what he needed to, even though it had made him late getting to Lola's.

But that was yesterday. This morning, he had a problem. It was clear from the photos they'd looked at last night, that he needed to get back into the flat and remove any evidence of the original dress ...and the portrait was potentially damning. He needed to get it. He waited in the café, until he was sure the apartment was empty again, then went up the stairs. After the fourth attempt to unlock the door failed, he realised that the locks had been changed. He was not happy. He would have to step up his plans.

Sofía and Pedro spent some time that morning, looking through Egnacio's files, trying to follow the list of 'repairs'.

It looked as if Pamela's theory about an illegal pawnshop was correct. Either that or Egnacio was the worst jeweller ever, as too many of the items were returned again and again, like clockwork.

Sofía had already decided that Egnacio's son needed further investigation. Frau Schmeckler still had to be questioned, but right now it would be best to speak to the Garcia family about the dress, and it was time they located and interviewed the seamstress. An officer from Madrid was going to send information about Valentina Karkoff with more up-to-date photos, but there were too many suspects and too many possible motives. It was starting to feel overwhelming.

Her instinct, however, said that neither Egnacio's son, Angel López, nor his wife had been responsible for killing him. It would have been like killing the golden goose and then pointing a neon sign saying 'Illegal Activity' at the business that had provided them a very comfortable lifestyle. Angel's voluntary visit to the station that morning saved them some time.

Sofía was convinced that Angel had been quick to grab the repairs after his father's death, because he wanted to carry on that lucrative side of the business.

Certainly, a forensic analysis of Egnacio's accounts showed that the Jewellery shop was running at a loss, apart from the declared income from repairs, and it was a fair bet that the records he kept for tax understated his income.

The undeclared side of the business must be much bigger.

It took barely an hour for Angel to break.

It only took another thirty minutes to extract everything he knew about his father's business.

As they thought, the pawn shop was a large element of Egnacio's illegal activity, but the most lucrative side was blackmail.

However, Angel had searched the shop and the account books from top to bottom and hadn't found either a list of victims or the hold his father had on them. He knew nothing about the origin of the kris, but he'd seen it in the display cabinet on his last visit. He'd noticed it because the wooden sheath was delicately carved – it was clearly an item of quality and value. He wondered if the kris could be returned to him after the investigation was concluded.

Sofía was speechless but, luckily, Angel didn't seem to notice and continued to talk at high speed; it was as if, having started, he couldn't stop.

He had three pieces of jewellery too many – or rather two because the third was the brooch they'd established as belonging to Frau Schmeckler. He had no record of it. There was also an ornate diamond necklace, with three stones missing and a bag of loose facetted crystals, of no particular value, neither of which showed on any receipt or invoice.

Without enough evidence to charge Angel with any criminal activity connected to his father and as he was co-operating fully with the police, there was no excuse to hold him, for now.

By the time Angel's statement had been written up and signed, the email from Madrid was waiting in Sofía's inbox. She called Pedro into her borrowed office to see the photos. He was not going to believe it! They both stared at the screened images of Valentina Karkoff. The small Asian woman who stared back at them was definitely not the seamstress they had seen in any other photos, nor anything like the woman described to them.

The email included Valentina's personal contact details, including her mobile phone, so Sofía dialled it, but had to leave a message. The recording promised a rapid reply, they would just have to hope it was telling the truth.

When Pamela, Sally and Raoul finished their light lunch, the bell from the church was sounding two o'clock. Sensing that Pamela and Sally needed to rest, Raoul went back into his apartment and left the two women in peace.

Pamela insisted on going into her studio to work. Sally understood her need to get back to normality as quickly as possible, but followed her into the studio space, to make sure she had everything she needed.

"Why have you moved the dress?" Pamela asked. She wasn't particularly upset, a lot had been going on and the painting was far enough advanced to reference the dress's position, so it was not important.

"I didn't!" Sally felt a bit aggrieved; she would never move one of her mother's painting props.

She moved behind the easel to look over Pamela's shoulder at the painting and then at the mannequin.

Her mother was right. Accepting that part of Pamela's skill as an artist was accuracy, the folds of the dress on the chair were not quite right. The crystals in the bodice also seemed duller, somehow.

How very strange.

They rearranged the skirt to mirror the position and folds that Pamela had painted on the canvas and when satisfied that all were in the right place, they went back to the easel.

Pamela looked on anxiously as Sally checked the stitching in the painting, comparing it to the real dress. There were tiny differences but, somehow, she knew it was important that Pamela did not alter her painting. If any detail was different now, it couldn't be the painting that had changed. Something was very wrong.

It took some persuasion, but Pamela finally agreed to wait until Pedro came later, before touching the painting. Dolores was not coming back for another sitting until next week, so she still had time to finish. Plus, Sally had some legitimate work for Pamela. Her boss had asked for some sketches of dancers for the magazine, to go with an article.

Secretly, Pamela was pleased to have something that she could do in the lounge, with her feet up. The few minutes of worry in the studio had been more stressful than she could have expected.

Sally went into her office and caught up with her work while Pamela sat with a box of pencils, a pad and a book describing dance moves, full of photos. She sketched away the rest of the afternoon, interrupted only by the occasional coffee.

The Garcia residence was a lovely traditional Spanish townhouse, near the church in the oldest part of the town. The entrance was an imposing pair of wooden doors set into what must once have been the archway entrance to a courtyard and carriage area. Now, however, it led into a large spacious hallway, through which Sofía and Pedro were led into an elegant drawing room.

Without doubt, the Garcia family was wealthy. This was what Pamela and Sally's house must have looked like in the days when it was all one home, thought Sofía, as she took stock of her surroundings.

Señor Garcia was delighted with their interest in the dress he'd commissioned for Dolores. He offered condolences for Pedro to convey to Pamela over the attack and saw no problem about the week's delay in the portrait. They'd received the dress earlier than expected, so a week would make little difference.

Being asked about the dress pleased him. He was delighted to tell them about the fair he'd attended in Madrid, with his wife and daughter. They'd gone to see the latest dresses designed by Valentina Karkoff and had been thrilled to hear that she was opening a studio in Puerto Amarillo.

Sofía had two printouts with her – one photo showed the real Valentina and the other the woman they had all thought was her. She showed both pictures to him and asked if he knew either of them.

"Oh yes, the Asian lady is Valentina, the other is her chief seamstress, Camilla, I am sorry, I don't know her last name. Valentina does all the designs, she asked Dolores what dress features she wanted, and Camilla made notes and showed us samples of the material. Valentina was incredible, she did the sketches while Dolores chatted about what she would like – it was how I imagine an artist sketch for you police is done, only it wasn't a face that Dolores was describing to her, it was her dream dress."

He paused and went to a drawer in the desk. Opening it, he removed a folder full of drawings and scraps of material. "These are the preliminary sketches she did, aren't they amazing?"

The dresses were quick, fluid, charcoal renditions of a young woman, standing in various poses, from different angles, wearing slightly different dresses. They were all clearly Dolores, based on the family photos on the wall.

"So," Sofía asked, "did you meet with Camilla here in the Port, for the fittings?"

"Oh, yes, Camilla brought the dresses to the house, for Dolores to try on. So much more convenient now that she is running a branch of the design studio from here. We confess we were surprised that Valentina didn't tell us she would be coming here."

"Señor Garcia, someone told me about your helping with the import of the material, can you tell me how you got involved?"

Señor Garcia looked puzzled by the question, "Oh, that was no bother, my cousin works in customs in Barcelona where the dresses and other raw materials are sent when they are imported from South America, India and China. Camilla told me that there had been a problem with some of the custom's seals being damaged in transit, but I rang my cousin, who inspected the boxes himself, and he couldn't see any difference between the inventory and the contents, so he was able to get the problem sorted very quickly." Before Sofía could interrupt with another question, he continued. "Camilla does a lot of the work on her own, she was very anxious that she was running out of time to meet her deadlines, there were the raw materials for several orders in the crates, I didn't do anything illegal, did I?"

As they were leaving, reasonably satisfied with all they'd learned, Pedro asked one more question "Sir, you said *dresses* for fitting, I thought the Reina only wore one dress?"

Señor Garcia laughed ruefully, "Camilla is a good saleswoman, as well as Valentina's top seamstress. She persuaded my wife that, with three weeks' worth of festivities, it might be wise to have a second dress in reserve, in case the first was soiled or damaged. She gave us a good discount and has arranged to buy both dresses back at the end of the fiesta at a third of what we paid, so she can cannibalise what she can retrieve into next season. I am happy with that, the dress will then be totally unique to my daughter. Even with the deal, it was still more than the last fiesta dress we bought, when our older daughter was Reina, six years ago. Valentina made that one too, that is when we first met Camilla, in Alicante, at an Exhibition." He looked happy, "I do love getting a bargain. I have copies of the receipts somewhere."

He rummaged in the drawer from which he'd taken the sketches. "Oh, here is Camilla's card with her contact details."

He handed them a business card and then the invoice and receipt from Valentina. "Why does the invoice show only one dress?" Sofía asked, her head buzzing as all the little pieces started to whirl round her head.

The pieces refused to settle, when he answered.

"Camilla said that was normal, the main dress included the spare, but they are identical, so just one design, so it only counts as one dress. The total amount *is* what I paid though, so nothing is fishy about the invoice, my gestor would be on it straight away if there was and he has already included it in my personal accounts, which is why I have the copy back."

Borrowing the invoice and taking the cards, they left. They needed to talk to Pamela about getting hold of the dress to have their suspicions checked.

When Roberto wandered into Lola's Café, at the end of his patrol, the café was quiet, and the tables cleared ready for lunch. He could hear voices in the kitchen. Lola was chatting to Angelica.

"So, you still haven't seen the designer, Valentina, upstairs yet?"

"Not hide nor hair, though I have met a couple of the hunky guys who did the move, if I were only ten years younger…" Angelica grinned.

"Hola Chico." Lola turned to Roberto giving him a big warm smile. She hadn't seen much of him since the murder, apart from the interviews, and she was dying to have him to herself for a bit. Angelica had just finished her cortado, so rose and left them to chat, going back into her shop.

"So, will you be able to get this evening off?" Lola asked. "I have help tonight, so I can finish early."

Roberto's answering nod and smile didn't reach his eyes. She could see it was going to be one of his moody days, where she needed to keep the conversation light and shallow. He had a real temper, her man, she certainly didn't want to provoke it. Best not to talk, let him say what he came to say, or at least to start the conversation.

She picked up the dirty coffee cups, smiling when she saw that Angelica had paid for both, a real friend, sweet, especially as she knew that she didn't need even to pay for her own.

Roberto followed her to the counter leaning, suggestively, against her as she reached across to the till, to pop in the coins. His desire was evident, she could feel him through the thin dress she wore, but she didn't feel comfortable with him being so obvious in public.

She turned away, wriggling out of his grasp as he tried to lick her ear. She wished he wouldn't do that; she didn't like it when he got so grabby – this was her café and she didn't want her customers to get the wrong idea.

Roberto laughed, he got quite a kick out of it when she resisted, he always won in the end, but the chase was always fun. Still, he would be moving on soon, so he had no problem pushing Lola a little harder. He had ambitions; in this respect he definitely took after his mother. Together, they were finally going to be able to make enough money to ditch Spain and start a new life somewhere where her skill and his less subtle talents, backed by some real money, were going to make a difference. He hated being in the police, but it had let him see the seamier side of life on the Costas. He'd certainly seen where money could be made, although it was his mother who'd come up with the idea, the contact and the goods!

He'd detested having to move to the Port, it was

too stifling a world, too small for him, too much like all the places he'd been sent when a kid, living with his father.

Growing up without a mother had been hard, his father was always too rigid, too old-fashioned and, in his last years, too drunk to be much of a parent. When he died, last year, though, Roberto's life had changed.

Apart from a few work colleagues, he'd felt alone and bereft at the crematorium. They'd all disappeared as soon as they decently could, leaving him sitting, on his own, in the bar he'd selected for a post-funeral toast.

After drinking and brooding for what felt like the entire evening, just as he finished his last drink, he'd felt a hand on his shoulder. Looking round he'd nearly fallen off his chair.

Apparently, his dead mother was talking to him.

Only she wasn't dead.

His father had lied.

All those years of grieving for her, of missing her, of feeling alone, she was alive, living in Madrid.

She told him that she'd tried to see him, she'd written and sent letters to him, but his father had stopped them, and her, and threatened to tell Roberto terrible lies about her, if she persisted.

The final compromise had been that she would get updates on his life once a year on Roberto's birthday, but she was not to see him again. If she didn't agree, she was risking going to prison, for something she'd done when he was little.

It was wonderful having her in his life, getting to

know her and having someone who cared for him, but saw him as he was. He hadn't understood, until she came back, how much he'd missed out on, not having a mother.

It was just as well his father was already dead, or he would have had to deal with him.

Poor mother. They had so much time to make up for, so much past to explore and now a future to plan.

He nuzzled Lola's neck, drinking in her trembling, scent and warmth.

Fear or longing, he didn't care that much, he just liked the feel of his power and her reaction.

More customers came into the café, it was gradually picking up for lunch so, reluctantly, Roberto knew he needed to leave Lola to her work. He murmured in her ear, that he needed to finish his rounds, but would be back for an 'early night'.

Slipping out of the back of the café, he checked there was no one near where he'd parked his car. Unlocking it, he got the bag from the boot and, making sure that the street was still clear, walked to the door next to Lola's service entrance.

He looked up and down the quiet road, one more time, then seeing no movement, apart from traffic moving up and down the main road that ran across the end of the empty street, used his key to open the back door to Valentina's 'new outlet'. He entered, quickly, locking the door behind him. Gripping the bag, he ran lightly and easily up the stairs with his prize.

Always Right

Chapter 23 – Friday Afternoon

Clearly, Frau Schmeckler was unhappy about receiving yet another visit from the police. She'd not expected this much attention when she and Marianne had agreed to help Egnacio and his friend.

If he hadn't known her secret, she would have stopped their involvement a while ago. Even when she'd taken the lead, as clearly the best placed of the four of them to mastermind everything that needed to be done, she'd not been happy. It was all too complicated, there were too many pawns in the game, too many unknowns.

It had worked well for five years, but she'd known, last year that it should have been their last score.

They'd made a lot of money and, if the others had reinvested it as wisely as she had, they could have stopped then, easily. They hadn't.

This _was_ going to be the last year.

Well, it would have to be the last year.

They were being closed down, whether they liked it or not. With Egnacio and Marianne dead, they couldn't carry on, even if they wanted to. Thinking of Marianne, made her want to cry again.

It was just like Marianne to remember Fritz's birthday. The chocolate box had been delivered, along with flowers and a card for Fritz, on the day that Marianne had died.

So sweet of her. She'd known how much Fritzy's mommy loved chocolate. Chocolate was bad for dogs, but they both knew that the chocolates were not really for him at all.

Right now, she needed to feel the strength that Marianne had always given her. She wandered through to the kitchen and took the box out of the fridge, opening it and putting it on the counter while she thought of her life now.

Maybe she should just walk away. Leave one remaining player to scoop this year's takings. She'd had enough, she didn't need anything else. She may have lost the one person who mattered most, but she still had Fritzy and a lifestyle she enjoyed. She was getting the brooch back, so nobody had any hold over her now.

As long as she could convince the police that the murders were nothing to do with her, she could take Fritzy for a nice little holiday. He loved the mountains. She would drive down to Andalucía with him, tonight, enjoy the wines, the cheap food and walks with her little Fritzy witzy. Before she left, she would tell her remaining partner that it was all hers and she was welcome to take the lot. Happy with her plans, she picked another chocolate out of the now half-empty box and popped it into her mouth as she headed to the door.

Right this moment, however, she had to get rid of the police!

When Sofía had shown Frau Schmeckler the photograph of her at the Exhibition, she'd been quite stunned. 'Doomed from the beginning' was all she could think at first.

After pressure, she agreed that she and Marianne had been friends for some time. She'd been staying with Marianne that weekend. The photo was taken just after she'd introduced her to Egnacio, having recognised him, by chance, at the event.

"Fritzy was just coming up to being one year old and Marianne wanted to buy me some jewellery to celebrate his birthday, so they got chatting and we walked to his stand to have a look at what he had on display."

"You and Marianne have been friends for a long while? How long? Did she get on well with your husband? When will Herr Schmeckler be back?"

The questions from the police seemed relentless, maybe because these were the questions that she did not want to answer.

The questions that exposed her life as the sham it was...

She had to tell them, they would find out anyway.

"Marianne and I have been close friends for nearly fifteen years. I don't care anymore; I don't care who knows. My husband and I divorced fourteen years ago and no, they did not get on, principally because I divorced him to be with her. So, he will never be back ...and now she won't be back, either!"

The tears wouldn't stop. She started to choke.

She couldn't talk

She couldn't breathe...

"Inhaler, my inhaler ...on the table ...please."

She grabbed the chair, gasping, shaking, clutching the tablecloth as she slid to the floor with it still gripped in her hand. The photo frames, the vase and everything else on the table crashed, smashed and scattered over her as she collapsed.

She clutched at her stomach, vomiting, cramping and mumbling between each spasm. The ambulance arrived before she lost consciousness, but all they could make out from her hoarse whispering were the words, *"Not Marianne... Chocolates! No, not Marianne... Only Egnacio knew..."*

Sofía's team from the Guardia searched the villa, thoroughly.

Because the word *chocolate* was one of the few distinguishable words they'd heard her say after her collapse, the open chocolate box was photographed in situ, then rushed to the lab.

With it, went a note that they should tell the hospital the type of poison, as soon as it was identified. It was strange that nobody, including the paramedics who'd attended, had any doubt that it was poison.

Sofía sat on the settee, trying to make notes, gather her thoughts and coordinate the forensic technicians.

When the team went upstairs to Frau Schmeckler's bedroom they found Fritz, whimpering with fear in her wardrobe. Wriggling past the technician, who tried to catch him, the small dachshund dashed straight down the stairs and leaped onto Sofía's lap, licking her face and hands as if she was the only friend he had left in the world.

Sofía was astonished, she vaguely remembered petting the dog on her first visit. Cute dog though. Maybe she would take him in for a few days, while they waited for his mistress to recover – if she recovered.

Before she left, she checked with the policeman who she had assigned to the Frau in the hospital. There was only a slim chance that she would pull through. They needed to know what the poison was, but the lab had still not got back to them. The doctor didn't expect her to survive. However, in the hope that she would, he'd arranged 24-hour cover for her security, with the local police, and left instructions that the sergeant would be notified if the Frau woke up. She would certainly not be back in the house for the next few days.

Sofía moved into the kitchen and picked up an empty supermarket bag. Checking that the technicians were happy for her to remove the tins and bowls they'd finished with, she put dog food, two dog bowls and a couple of his toys in the bag and headed for the car with the bag, the dog and his lead.

She drove back home with Fritz curled up on the floor beside her. He slept fitfully; small whimpers alternated with the movements of his tail as it periodically thumped the car's floor.

On her way past Lola's, she glanced down the street behind the café. She was driving slowly, stuck behind a tourist who was clearly lost and moving at snail's pace.

With a good view down its full length, from the main road, it would have been difficult not to see Roberto walking furtively, along the road behind the café.

Odd. Perhaps he'd parked there.

He was a strange man, not a bit like Pedro or any of the other local police that she'd met. For a start, he wasn't from the town, he'd only moved there a few months ago.

Pedro had commented that Roberto embraced neighbourhood patrol as a way to meet women, so he would be surprised if Lola was his only girlfriend, but Sofía sensed that Pedro didn't really like Roberto much.

She dismissed the thought, distracted by the tourist in front who braked suddenly to avoid a pedestrian, foolish enough to think that a zebra crossing was a safe place to cross the road. Clearly a tourist...

Sally had left a message for Pedro to please call in, if he had time, but she knew that he'd be busy catching up on his work. He'd spent a lot of time with her yesterday.

When the doorbell rang, her hands were full of books that she was moving out of her office. Pushing them into a teetering pile on the hall table, she smoothed back her hair and opened the door, expecting to see Pedro. Raoul grinned at her, waving a bottle of Cava while gesturing behind him where Carlos, looking a little sheepish, was locking up their apartment door.

"Everything is fine, we are going out to celebrate, but we thought that you and Pamela might like to join us with Cava first."

"How lovely, yes of course," turning from the door as they entered, Sally called to her mother "Mother, Raoul and Carlos are here, we are going onto the balcony for a drink, are you coming?"

They grabbed glasses from the kitchen on their

way and were soon sitting in the sunshine.

"What are we celebrating?" Pamela asked as she settled into one of the cushioned seats, accepting a glass from Carlos.

"Well, it was meant to be a secret, for a few days longer, but Raoul was getting into a real tizz," Carlos smiled. "Pedro caught up with me yesterday and gave me a proper ticking off, said that poor Raoul thought I was leaving him, or at the very least, having an affair!"

Sally didn't know where to look at this, as she'd been convinced that the news about Carlos would not make Raoul happy.

Raoul caught her look and giggled, "don't worry, Sally, it's all good, it really is!"

Carlos grinned "It was all my fault! I was worrying about our five-year anniversary, I wanted to do something special, but I wanted it to be a big surprise and needed to save some extra cash. So, about two months ago I stopped taking the taxi back from Alicante and took the minibus that runs up and down the coast, instead. Every trip has saved me over 50 Euros, but I have been taking the taxi fare out of housekeeping, as normal, so that Raoul wouldn't suspect anything!"

He looked ruefully at Raoul. "I rather got that wrong, didn't I? I never really thought that anyone would make much of the extra hour it took, because there was almost always someone to drop off or pick up, but the taxi often used to get caught up with traffic."

Pamela refilled his glass and asked, "So what were you saving for and what are you both looking so happy about?"

"This!" Raoul slid his hand from below the table, where it had been resting, lightly on Carlos's thigh, and displayed it to them both. A black tungsten ring sparkling with rainbow coloured stones, flanked by small diamonds, caught the sunlight as he waved his hand, towards them, palm down.

"Ahh, how lovely Raoul – really lovely," breathed Sally, as she looked at them both, smiling.

Carlos laughed, "Of course, once Raoul said yes, it meant that I could go back to the jewellers, this morning, for the matching ring, for me! See!" He too showed off a ring.

"But that's not all, "said Raoul, happily, "Carlos booked a cruise, for our honeymoon, isn't it amazing! He has arranged everything, a civil ceremony by the mayor, a reception at la Casita Restaurant on the beach, we just need to issue our invitations." He solemnly handed each of them a colourful card. On the front was a selfie of Carlos and Raoul, with blue skies and the sea, behind them. "I did the cards, myself, while Carlos went to the jewellers. We took the photo on our first date together, so it seemed perfect."

Carlos interrupted, "Perfect? More like superb! So, will you both be free, Saturday week?"

Raoul added, saucily, "Pedro is coming. So?"

Pamela laughed, "Of course we will come, wouldn't miss your wedding for the world, would we Sally?"

Sally just blushed and agreed.

"Oh Sally, would you do me the honour of being our one and only bridesmaid, please?"

"Of course, Raoul, I would be honoured, as long as you're not planning for me to wear bright pink or orange!"

"Good grief woman, of course not! Carlos and I will be the only ones wearing the bright colours there, else how will we stand out from the rest of you? You can wear something drab and grey, so we will be the centre of attention on all the photos!" Sally's jaw dropped as she stared at Raoul, then she saw the start of a grin and the four of them just collapsed with laughter.

Pedro's day was not going smoothly. His visit to the tourist office was frustrating. Apparently, Roberto had already been in and reviewed all the CCTV footage, that morning. He had told the technician that there was nothing worth saving, so the disk had been cleaned ready to reuse.

Pedro was seething. Setting aside the waste of his time and that Roberto had not told either Sofía or him what he'd done, the opportunity to eliminate people by their absence was as important as including a suspect by their presence. Roberto had no right to allow the hard drive to be formatted without her having a chance to see for herself. Roberto must be the most incompetent policeman he'd ever met. Too bad he was now messing up the murder enquiry.

He was sick of covering for him.

Even worse, someone would have to tell the boss and break it to Sofía. Unless, he told the Jefe and let him tell her. That might be a clever idea, but *NO,* he was tougher than that. He called Sofía.

Chapter 24 – Friday Evening

It was obvious to the doctors that, with the German's age, weight and pre-existing heart problems, any condition that wracked her body like this was putting their patient in severe danger, so they were very reluctant to stress her even more by giving the police access to her.

On the other hand, the police lab had confirmed it was ricin poisoning - very nasty and deliberate.

Ironically, her best chance of survival was because it had been ingested, not injected or inhaled.

This had also reduced the chances of cross contamination. However, there was still a risk.

All the attending officers and medical staff had been collected together and brought in for decontamination.

Every single thing, person and place they had been in contact with since leaving the villa was also put under scrutiny. In some cases, like Sofía's, as she had gone off duty, this had included her home, her husband, baby Rosa and their new four-legged house guest. As the victim's pet, the dog had received special attention and because they'd both been in direct contact with the Frau, he'd travelled with her to the unit for a really thorough check.

The clothing worn by everyone who had come near the Frau had been isolated, along with anything else that might have come into contact with them. Everything inanimate had been sealed and removed and a decontamination unit had been sent in by the Military Emergencies Unit (UME) team from the *Tercer Batallón de Intervención en Emergencias* as a precaution.

Sofía had not been thrilled to spend the next few hours being prodded poked, showered and decontaminated before being allowed to resume her life as a wife and mother.

Still, she was glad that they were taking precautions, even if this was clearly a criminal rather than terrorist act. As soon as she was clear, she rang her husband's mobile. He and Rosa had also had to go through decontamination procedures, so he was considerably shaken.

It had been a tearful conversation as the enormity of the unseen risk she had been exposed to finally struck her. Her job had put her baby in danger! But then, as her husband told her, it was doing her job that stopped risks like this one from being commonplace. She really loved that man; he was the most wonderful man in the world.

Next, she rang Pedro and updated him, making sure that he warned the Wrights that they could also be in danger and might be targeted, so must be careful. She then spent an hour on the phone, reassuring her boss that she was not only OK, but within a whisker of closing the case. Not that she was, but it had sounded convincing.

Finally, she was free to go home and confirm that her husband didn't hold her responsible, and to hug Rosa.

Before she left, she was a little surprised to be handed a bag with new bowls and a dog lead inside – Fritzy, she had totally forgotten the dog!

To her relief, the woman with the bag was followed by another carrying a very bewildered, damp and fresh-smelling dachshund.

Fritzy, cleared to go, was still her problem. No way was she carrying him so, fishing the lead from the bag and attaching it to the dog, they both wandered out into the warmth of the evening.

As she walked to her car, she realised that the reason why she had never seen it so clean before was, probably, because it had never been so clean, at least not since it was in the factory – and maybe not even then. The decontamination team had been thorough.

She had never been so frightened, in her life and she didn't like it.

Still, while it was making her focus, it didn't stop her from making a wry mental note to check the name of the car decontamination crew to see if they did any off-book valeting.

By the time Pedro finished his reports and caught up with Sofía's news, he ought to have been too tired to want to socialise. On the other hand, he did worry that Pamela, Sally and her Gran might be in danger.

With messages and texts from both Raoul and Sally, he really should go to see them both.

He called ahead and was pleased to discover they were both at Pamela's, the tinto was open, cava was on ice and more than enough paella was on order to feed him as well.

A much better idea than brooding the evening away on his own. "That sounds as if you're celebrating something," he commented, but neither Sally nor Raoul would spill the secret they wanted to share with him. "I'll pick up Cha-Cha, give her a run and then bring her round, if I may?"

"Of course, we'll be glad of the extra company and mother would like your opinion on something." Sally smiled as she put the phone down, then went into the kitchen to sort out the extra plate, glass and cutlery.

By the time Pedro arrived, after his run with Cha-Cha and a shower, not only did he feel reinvigorated, but the paella had been delivered and was just about to be served.

He sipped wine and watched Sally laughing and eating and felt himself starting to unwind. Sitting in good company and listening to Raoul and Carlos chatting about their plans for the wedding was helping him to relax far quicker than he'd expected. He dreaded breaking the mood with his news, but neither Raoul nor Carlos had any need to know, yet, so why ruin their evening? There was no talk of murder or the investigation until the meal was cleared away and Raoul and Carlos bade goodnight and went back to their flat.

Pamela was clearly quite tired, so Pedro was surprised when, before he had a chance to speak, she asked Sally to bring Pedro into the studio, to show him the dress. "I have seen it Pamela. It's very beautiful, so what's the problem?"

"We don't know, but Sally and I are convinced that

something is wrong …different." She walked across to the studio and Pedro followed, bemused. He and Sofía had talked about the dress and theorised about how it might tie into the murders, but it was all very tenuous. So, what had changed?

The studio area was equipped with several high wattage 'daylight' bulbs and a strong neon strip light. Pamela flipped the switches, so that the painting and the dress were clearly lit.

"Can you see it?" Sally asked, as she joined them. "Something has changed since the morning mother was hurt. Look at the painting and then look at the dress."

Pedro stood where Sally indicated, behind the easel, in the spot where Pamela sat to paint. From there he could see both the painting and the dress clearly.

He knew, instinctively, that it was not the slight change in position, from where he'd first seen the painting and dress a few days ago, that was the problem.

The vibrance in the painted jewels had always had more sparkle than the original, but now it was even more noticeable. The richness on the canvas that he'd also seen in the dress, attracting both his and Sofía's attention, was no longer reflected in real life.

Then he noticed the pattern of the crystals sewn around the neck of the gown; in the painting it was different from the gown on the chair. In the painting there were eleven crystals, placed evenly around the neckline, nestling in the lace, with the largest in the centre. On the dress, itself, he could only count nine.

The arrangement was the same but the gap between each crystal was larger. Even with Pedro's brief acquaintance with Pamela, he knew that this was not a mistake she would have made, she was far too meticulous.

Armed with this thought, he then checked the sleeves and the bodice. There were definitely fewer crystals on the dress on the chair than in the painting.

Even more odd was that the crystals were duller than he remembered. They just didn't catch the light in the same way as the ones he'd seen before.

He fished out his phone and went back through shared folder of photos that he and Sofía had taken when they'd each seen the dress first. Eleven stones decorated the neckline of the dress in all the photos.

The sparkle was in the photos, but no longer in the stones on the dress in the studio. Without question, this was NOT the same dress.

"Yes, I can see it. I need to ring Sofía, this is important. When did you first notice that the dress was different?" Pedro asked.

"When we came back from the hospital. The first time mother went into the studio, we had to rearrange the mannequin," Sally answered. "Raoul said that after we left to follow mother to the hospital, he and Sofía came into the flat, briefly, and they both looked around to make sure that no one had been in. I think he said that she took another couple of photos of the dress. Why are you both so interested in it? And why and how has it been swapped for one that's almost identical? What will we tell the Garcias? What can this possibly have to do with Egnacio's murder?

Was this why mother was attacked?"

"Breathe *Cariña*, breathe." Pedro drew her to him
and held her gently as she sobbed out her questions.
"At the moment, we are guessing. We need evidence
and yes, right now I believe the dress may have been
the motive for the attack on Pamela – but until it
happened, we'd no idea that Pamela was in danger
or that anyone was after the dress. It doesn't make
sense. I rather thought that their plan would be to
wait until after the fiesta and the dress had been
worn. We thought that it was a plan they'd followed
elsewhere ...so the Garcia family might later have
been in some danger, but not Pamela! We were
obviously wrong."

He walked her gently back into the sitting room
and, having made sure that Pamela was OK, went
onto the balcony, to phone Sofía.

From the sofa, Sally and Pamela could only hear
Pedro's side of the conversation, but it was enough
for them to fill in some of the gaps. "Sofía, *hablamos
ingles por favor*. I am at Pamela and Sally's place, I
think it would help if they can hear what I say, now."
Pedro turned and smiled at them both. "*Gracias*, OK.
Can you remember what time it was, please, when
you and Raoul came into their apartment and you
photographed the dress? ...As soon as we'd gone?
...OK, well, between then and now, someone has used
a set of keys to enter their apartment and remove
the dress... Yes, we had the locks changed last night,
but we don't know if the dress was replaced before
or after the lock was changed. We know that it was
only noticed today, after Pamela came home. Yes,
truly, the dress has been swapped, I think for the

'spare' that Garcia told us about... Yes... *Si*... No, the flat has not been broken into and Raoul had Sally's old and new keys, safe. Yes, Pamela's old keys were picked up by the ambulance driver and, apparently, they were brought to the police station. No, they haven't been returned to Pamela, yet... I'll check." He turned to Pamela and asked, "Are there any more sets of keys to your flat?"

Pamela shook her head and checked to see if Sally had also picked up the significance of Pedro's comment. She had.

Pedro returned to his call. "No Sofía, apart from Pamela's missing old set and any the locksmith may have kept back of the new, all are accounted for. OK, will do... No, I think that the thief has already taken the only thing that they wanted from here, but until I can get another locksmith out, I'll stay here. *Si*, I will use a different one, just in case."

Pedro made another couple of calls and then came back in to sit down, on the sofa next to Sally.

"OK," he said, "I've asked George to pop round. He's our local locksmith; we use him a lot from the station. He is English, but he grew up in the port. We were at school together. His family has been here for forty years or so, so he is almost Spanish." He grinned. "Once you have new locks, I will leave you both to it. Sofía is organising a visit to the Garcias, in the morning, to find out where the spare dress was kept, as whoever had access to it has to be at the top of the list."

"I can tell you where the other dress was kept" offered Pamela. "The dressmaker was holding it until the fiesta started, remember, it is a spare, so may never be needed or worn."

"All trails keep leading back to Valentina Karkoff, don't they? She has to know something." Sally said.

"Which one? The real Valentina or whoever, here, has been using her name?" asked Pedro.

They both gaped at him.

"Please understand that this is for your ears only, I'll be in real trouble if the Sarge finds out I'm sharing what little I know, with you, but I think we are going to need your help to get this sorted. Plus, you have been targeted and without your photos we wouldn't be as far ahead as we are."

Sally grabbed a fresh bottle of red wine and, while she opened it and refilled their glasses, Pedro brought them up to date with everything he knew, that he didn't think Sofía would kill him, for telling them. It was a fine line, but he didn't want Sally to be at risk and pooled knowledge was usually the best defence.

The main points that worried all of them were...

Might the poisoner target them?

Why hadn't the real Valentina Karkoff contacted the police?

Was Camilla the same person as the fake designer using Karkoff's name? The faker was, apparently, being very successful at it, so it would explain her access to Valentina's designs and how she had the skills to copy them. If so, why would a legitimate employee, from a top line successful studio, be involved in switching dresses or possibly be connected to the murders?

How were the keys taken from the police station?

Who took them and how was that person going to cover for the disappearance?

Sally was about to suggest that she could have a chat with Lola and her seamstress friend, in the morning, when Cha-Cha, who'd snoozed most of the evening away, suddenly started up, growling. The doorbell rang. George had arrived to change the locks on the apartment and on the storage unit.

When he finished, he gave Pamela three pairs of keys for the two doors with a new lock. He'd installed a Chubb and a Yale on each door. "I know the flat is yours, so that extra set is a spare – but the third set, for the storage unit door, needs to go to whoever rented it to you. Legally, they have a right to have access to that part of the property, as they own it."

Pedro and Sally looked at each other – the shops next to Lola's were all rented – would the same apply to their owners, or were they all owned by the same person?

After George had been paid and gone back to his van, Pedro called Cha-Cha from her chosen bed (the easy chair nearest the studio) and, regretfully, after a brief embrace, that they both wished was longer, left Sally to lock up behind him.

It was clear that, Saturday or not, Pedro would be working tomorrow."

Chapter 25 – Saturday Morning

Roberto woke to the clattering sound of his alarm. Four-thirty in the morning on a Saturday, *why had he set an alarm that early?*

Oh yes.

Original plan – get the dress, swap it back and then they'd disappear. No one any the wiser. He would drop the Wright's keys on the floor of the station, near the counter – then leave to start his long-booked holiday.

Now, he still needed to swap the dress, but was going to have to break in and fake a robbery. One more rotten complication in his life.

If all went well, they wouldn't even know he was gone for the first two weeks and, by then, he and his mother would have vanished.

First things first, he needed to get dressed and see what was happening at the hospital with the German woman. Marianne was always going on about her friend's love of chocolates, there was enough ricin in that box to down an elephant, she should be dead by now.

What should he wear in hospital, on a Saturday, so as not to draw attention? Uniform or non-uniform?

Nobody suspected him, so maybe uniform – it would get him through any security they may have set up – or at least close enough to see the lie of the land. He'd take a change of clothes with him for after though, as any of his colleagues, on guard at the hospital. would know he wasn't on duty.

This early in the morning, there'd be no top brass around. The hospital staff would be issuing first meds and sorting meals, so maybe he'd have a clear run.

It was six-thirty by the time he found free parking at the hospital, this was important as the official carpark not only charged, it photographed the registration plates of all vehicles entering the underground area.

It took another few minutes to find the volunteer desk where foreigners got help with translations from other foreigners who spoke Spanish and English or German or Russian or whatever heathen tongue they spoke.

He was in luck, the woman at the desk was new.

He spoke in Spanish, of course. There was no point in standing out any more than necessary.

"Excuse me, I wonder if you can help me, I have been called in to take a statement from a German patient, I left all the details back in my car, I was wondering who the translator was and if they'd any info on her for me? It would be a real help, I had to park right on the other side of the hospital and my appointment is in about five minutes." He smiled his best *'boyish charm' look* at the middle-aged volunteer.

She melted, as he'd hoped she would.

"Can you remember the patient's name? I can look in the diary"

He gave Schmeckler's name and waited while she checked her diary. "No, nothing for today, but she has a German-Spanish translator booked for Monday in Room 1104 at eleven in the morning. Is it possible you have the wrong day?"

"Oh dear, how stupid of me – all that walk for nothing, thank you though – looks like I'll see you the day after tomorrow"

He smiled politely at her and walked away, towards the wards.

So, she was alive! Damn – and would be awake enough to talk by Monday, assuming that she hadn't talked already. He'd best find Room 1104, fast!

After breakfast, Sally made sure that she swapped all her 'old' keys for the newest of the new ones, before she left the flat. She dropped the second new set of keys and all three storeroom keys into her mother's handbag and stored the third set of flat keys in the key cupboard they'd hidden in the kitchen. She was reluctant to let her mother wake up to an empty flat, but she put the coffee machine on, so at least Pamela would know that she'd thought of her.

There was something therapeutic about walking down the main stretch of the port in the gentle heat of the morning, before the shops and businesses opened. It was quiet, apart from a stray cat that skulked out of a cool dark alleyway to stretch itself out on a sun-warmed step.

By the time she'd reached the seafront, the Saturday morning market stands were out, lined up along the pedestrian way. She lingered for a while, admiring the artisan wares that were being set out.

It would be an hour before Lola opened, so she'd given herself plenty of time to amble and browse and just enjoy the atmosphere.

It was a strange sensation, she'd been here too long now to be a tourist, but not quite long enough to get over the novelty of this being her home.

She was pleased that her ear was beginning to define the Spanish words being spoken around her, although she still understood so few. Even just a few days of being around Pedro had helped her start to really listen, instead of just letting the Spanish wash over her. Just absorbing the words used in context was a help. Like the little girl dragging an old lady from stall to stall, saying *'Abuelita!'*, repeatedly, to attract her grandma's attention to a new trinket, or the old man who muttered, *'Guapa, guapa'* underneath his breath every time a pretty young girl walked past the bench where he sat, enjoying the view.

Well they were two words she would probably remember, she smiled to herself.

There was a stall full of tablecloths, very similar to the ones Lola used, which reminded her of where she was meant to be. Before she left the last of the stalls, she couldn't resist buying a perfumed soap for her mother. Pamela liked putting scented soaps in the drawers where she kept her blouses – it gave the room and clothes a freshly laundered smell.

By the time she got to Lola's, the tables were all set out and Lola was sitting at the bar watching her brother take care of the first few morning clients.

They exchanged hugs and fake-kissed both cheeks – normal for old friends here and Sally settled

175

down next to her, deliberately facing the sea with her back to Egnacio's. She looked at her friend, the first real friend she'd made in the town, after coming to live here, and was immediately concerned. There were dark smudges under Lola's eyes, and she was sure she could see the edge of a bruise on her arm, covered by most of her sleeve.

"Are you OK Lola, who has hurt you?"

Lola self-consciously tugged her sleeve down to try and hide the bruise better. "It is nothing, Sally, it was an accident, I am sure."

"Roberto?"

"Yes. Roberto!" José's voice from behind Sally sounded tense with suppressed anger, "I have not seen him since I saw my sister, but I will be ready for him. You need to denounce him Lola, policeman or not, there are strong laws against abuse here in Spain."

Sally was indignant, she'd no idea that Roberto was such a swine. "You must say something, to someone, before José does anything silly."

She hugged Lola, properly this time, and felt her wince. "I am sorry, Lola. Here sit down and tell me what happened. What do you really know about Roberto? I know he's a policeman, but where I come from, not all policemen are perfect."

"Yes, Lola, what do you know about Roberto?" Pedro joined them at the table, signalling to José to bring out some wine, "...and Sally, some policemen really are perfect!" He grinned so wickedly, that even Lola gave a small smile.

"Sorry if I startled you both, but I was on my way to ask you about Roberto, anyway. Why are you asking, Sally?"

José answered for her, as he put four glasses on the table and drew up a chair to join them. "He hurt my sister, Pedro, so you need to get to him before I do. I've never liked him, even if he has been good for information to impress my friends, he has told me stuff about the investigation, that I am sure he shouldn't. You would never have told me about the bodies and what they looked like, would you Pedro? Even if I'd begged you to, you would have said it was police business. Roberto was full of it and how important he was and how he was too important to stay long in a little place like Puerto Amarillo. He's always going on about how important he will be when he moves on, with his mother."

Pedro's head whipped round and he stared intently at the boy. "His mother? He doesn't know his mother, I've seen the files, she abandoned him as a kid. To all intents and purposes, he's an orphan. His father died a few months before he came here"

"Well he definitely said he was going places with his mother. She has just come into some money and he's going away with her, as soon as he can!"

"Do you know her name, José?" asked Sally and, when he shook his head, added "Does she live in the port with him?"

"She didn't, when I met Roberto." chipped in Lola, unhappily, "but I think she might have just moved here. I did wonder if she might be connected with the new dress designer's place. Roberto does seem to hover around the place more, since the seamstress moved in. Even Angelica has commented that she's seen more of him than she has of the new owner. I was getting a little jealous, I haven't seen the new designer yet, so I asked Roberto, last night, if she was young and pretty. That is when he hurt me, he shook me, hard, and told me to mind my own business!"

For a minute, she struggled not to cry then, giving up, sobbed out the awfulness of it. "She must be his mistress, not his mother. He has her keys, he visits her after he has spent the evening with me, I know he does, I hear him leave and a few minutes later, I hear someone running up the stairs next door."

Sally hugged her and over Lola's shoulder, watched Pedro and José exchange looks. She knew what that look meant, it needed no Spanish to interpret it. They were going to go next door and find out what was happening. "Whatever you both do, Pedro, I really think that you should let Sofía know first, she's already upset with Roberto, she also has been trying to get hold of the seamstress. She asked us all about her and, from what little you've told me, I think she might want to be present when you go next door."

José looked mulish, but Pedro grinned, saying, "You are very clever, *Cariña*. Yes, if I tell Sofía how Roberto has been behaving and what he has been saying, I think we'll get her blessing to go and look. It's Saturday and she's with her family for the first free time she has had in days, so she won't come, but our 'visit' will be sanctioned. I'll ring her now, José, then you and I will go explore."

He grabbed his phone and rang Sofía's mobile number, before anyone else spoke and complicated his life even more.

They watched him gesticulate as he paced up and

down in front of the restaurant, talking to the Guardia sergeant and listening to her responses some of which obviously surprised him. He frowned periodically, as he absorbed whatever she was saying, it made him look older and a little stern, Sally thought. She liked how expressive his face was, she felt she would know, straight-away, if he ever lied to her, he was open, honest, so different from Greg.

When Pedro came back inside, he sat for a few minutes savouring the glass of wine he'd left to make the call. Then he looked at the three of them patiently waiting to hear what he had to say.

Sally could see he was torn and was sure he shouldn't be telling them anything, so she was pleased when he muttered something impolite in Spanish, apologised and then swore them all to secrecy. He was about to tell them whatever it was he wasn't supposed to be telling them.

He started with how they must not go next door.

Chapter 26 – Granny Em's Wicked Day

It was no good, she felt *really* guilty.

Thursday night had been a natural follow-on from a wonderful day spent up in the mountains, above Guadalest.

By the time they had driven up, down, around and up again, it had been too late to drive back down the mountain in the dark. Miguel apparently 'stumbled' across an ancient Taberna, but his ruse was exposed as soon as the owner greeted him enthusiastically by name.

Somehow, he'd organised it so that they were the only people in the restaurant. After cocktails, heady wine and good company, the evening had ended in the owner's only guest room, drinks on the balcony and the sound of someone down in the valley below them playing romantic Spanish guitar music.

It had all been truly perfect; age didn't matter. Companionship and shared memories did the rest. But Em woke on Friday morning with a dreadful headache, more aches and pains than she could count and feeling every one of her numerous decades.

Miguel had risen early. She could hear him in the restaurant below, chatting to the owner's wife as she organised breakfast. Emma was grateful for the time to wash and change, but she was even more delighted to have the privacy to repair some of time's ravages to her face and to sort and take the various tablets and painkillers that she needed to face the day.

While in the bathroom, she noticed that Miguel had a similar collection of pills and lotions to hers. She took comfort from the notion that he had probably been as pleased as she was to have privacy, first thing in the morning.

It was funny they'd both carried several days' worth of tablets and potions with them. Almost as if they had both hoped, subconsciously, that the trip might be extended. Well, if he asked, she would consider it.

Breakfast was ready to be served by the time she managed to get downstairs. She'd left the luggage, packed, in their room, she would worry about that later. What he had ordered was absolutely right. Nothing too heavy for her 'morning after the night before' stomach, just toast and a light fluffy omelette and a mug that looked as big as a bucket, full of hot but milky coffee, fancy his remembering that!

When they finished, as she'd hoped, he suggested that they continue their tour farther south, how could she say no?

OK, she felt a little guilty, but she really didn't think that either Pamela or Sally would begrudge her feeling truly loved and happy for the first time in so many years ...and with her toy boy too! Well he was six months younger, so nearly a toy boy!

She grinned, she was happy, really, truly, absolutely happy.

So, it might not last.

It might fizzle as quickly as it blossomed, but perhaps not. Time enough to worry later if it did.

Miguel was ecstatic, every plan and arrangement he'd made, as soon as he heard that she was coming to visit her family, had worked perfectly.

Emma hadn't changed a jot; she was just as impulsive and mad as she always had been.

OK she was older, but so was he. He had always turned to Marta first, he loved his wife really and deeply, as Emma had Frank, but when Marta and Frank were no longer with them, he and Emma comforted each other. As a foursome they had been awesome; as the remaining couple, they consoled each other, filling the aching gaps left by their mutual losses. Life wouldn't be the same with Emma as it had been with Marta, but it would be so much better with Emma than with anyone else. He just hoped that, after a few days together, she would feel the same.

Whatever happened next, it was wonderful to have some time together, to feel alive again.

Next stop, the *Plaza Bocagrande* in Cartagena, where they could eat overlooking the sea and he could tell her stories of the founding of the port, two hundred years before the birth of Christianity. She would also be fascinated that the Spanish Navy were still using the base that took fifty years to build in the Eighteenth Century.

Maybe, if the day went well, he could persuade her to continue the trip even longer, up into the mountains of Andalucía.

When, over a late romantic lunch, he asked to extend their break even longer, Emma was pleased.

How could she not agree, she didn't want the trip to end either, although she insisted on exploring the shops in the Plaza, first, so she could replenish her meagre wardrobe. A woman might enjoy being swept off her feet, but a change of shoes and sparkly fresh, new underwear were also pretty important at her time of life!

Whilst he waited for the bill, she nipped into a nearby boutique to buy "the essentials". Meeting up again, outside the restaurant, they decided to spend a little time exploring the Mall. Miguel followed her around the shops, chatting as they window-shopped and patiently waiting when she saw something interesting. He seemed to be happy to discuss her choices and delighted in her pleasure when she fell in love with a stylish embroidered blouse even though that meant a new skirt, which led to another summery top...

She was in the car before she finally remembered to switch her phone on, to text Sally that she was OK, there was no signal, so none of Sally's messages about the attack on Pamela interrupted her romantic interlude and none of Pamela's later messages, about how she was really OK, arrived to reassure her.

Chapter 27 – Frau Schmeckler's Morning

The last thing that Frau Schmeckler could remember was that pretty young sergeant talking to her as she was lifted into the ambulance and promising to take care of Fritzy for her.

She'd been in agony, passing in and out of consciousness, between spasms of pain and vomiting, until she was eventually put on a drip and the pain gradually lessened.

Waking frequently during the night, she found herself hooked up to more and more machines, until the pain eased into something that allowed her to start thinking and remembering.

Each time she surfaced she felt Marianne's presence and, twice, thought that she saw her concerned face watching over her.

It was all very muddled.

The dopamine and isotonic fluid drip were having a positive effect and she would need to remain 'nil by mouth' for the next few days. The activated charcoal they had flushed through her system, as soon it was confirmed that it was ricin poisoning, seemed to have been effective. Everything she was wearing had been decontaminated – and they were isolating everything she'd touched as well as the clothes of everyone who had been near her.

Their biggest concern, aside from the need to eliminate the poison from her system, was the dysrhythmia it was causing, her heart.

Giving her any emetics to clear her stomach, besides being too late, would have been almost as dangerous as allowing the residue to remain. After the charcoal had done its work, it would be better for the poison to pass through her system and be disposed of, safely, once it 'exited'.

The bottom line was that there was no antidote.

The only cure was time.

The longer she stayed alive and her immune system fought the toxin, the better were the chances of her living and ultimately recovering, as much as she ever would.

The critical point would be the fifth day, if she got through it there was a chance she would live.

The doctor who phoned Sofía was able to tell her that the dosage had been small, but he warned her that very little ricin was needed to kill. It was surprising that they didn't see more ricin poisonings, it was too easy to grow the plant in Spain. Frau Schmeckler's height and the fact that she was a little overweight might tip the balance in her favour.

It was astonishing that she wasn't already dead. If she'd been small or frailer, she would have been, by now. She had been incoherent for most of the time since arriving in hospital but the German paramedic on the ambulance reported that every time the patient surfaced, she had cried out the same phrase. "Tell Camilla... The chocolates weren't from Marianne."

Sofía was clear in her own mind, that the Frau and Marianne had been up to something illegal involving jewellery. It seemed unlikely that Marianne had sent the poisoned chocolates and then been murdered by someone else. She needed to establish a timeline of events. When had the gift arrived and when had German woman started to eat them?

She'd watched, the day before, as the Forensic Team carefully emptied the kitchen rubbish bin. The Frau was clearly not very good at sorting her rubbish and separating waste food, paper and plastics.

The discarded packaging and gift-wrapping paper for the chocolate box was above Thursday's copy of the Bild Newspaper and underneath Fritzy's empty can of food from Thursday night. There was no stamp or courier information on the outer paper – nothing to indicate the origin, they would have to assume it was delivered by the killer sometime in the afternoon. Unfortunately, it was small enough to have gone into the Frau's mailbox, it didn't need to have been signed for.

Sofía checked the photos of the chocolate box. It was obvious from the top layer of paper wrappings that several chocolates had been eaten before they arrived, but she'd heard that, with ricin poisoning, it could take several hours for the first symptoms to show.

It meant that anyone could have been responsible for sending the poisoned chocolates. Worse, nobody's alibi mattered. There was no definite timeframe for when the chocolates had been delivered and only a rough indication of when they had been opened, before Fritzy's meal, the night before.

It was reassuring that the doctor was willing to work with the police to protect the patient from any more attempts to kill her, but she would not be in a fit state to answer questions until at least Monday, if she survived that long.

There would be a local policeman at her side, however, recording her mumbling, in case anything more of interest emerged. It would be useless in court, as it could not be presented, in any way, as a statement taken under legal advice, but it might give them a lead to stopping an attack on anyone else.

Picking up her tablet, Sofía browsed through the photos from Pamela. It was uncanny that three of the four people snapped, chatting in Alicante six years ago, had been attacked in the last three days. What had escalated it? Why now, after all this time?

At least they were now sure that the fourth person was Karkoff's seamstress, Camilla.

It was a fair bet that she was the woman Angelica spoke of to Lola. She needed to find out, once and for all, what game Camilla might be playing, not coming forward to make a statement while her 'friends' if that's what they were, were dying and being attacked.

Unless she'd gone into hiding because she was afraid, she would be next ...or had she disappeared because she was already a victim? Unfortunately, they had no more grounds for a search warrant at the workshop than for any other house in the Port.

What was left of the *Corcuera* Law (that she would need to invoke to search the apartment without a judge's warrant) was strictly confined to suspected drug trafficking and she really had no evidence that drugs were part of this equation.

There was only a tenuous link between Camilla and the ricin attack.

Worse, even if she could get a judicial warrant for a search of the premises, Camilla would need to be present, for the results of the search to be usable in any prosecution.

The paperwork for the search had been with the court since the day after the murder, but she still hadn't had the go-ahead.

Sofía still had no idea where Camilla was staying, despite many enquiries. Neither her mobile phone nor the workshop landline was being answered. She had even checked with Karkoff's personnel manager, who insisted that Camilla had not been in touch since the night Egnacio was killed.

On the bright side, he had relayed that Karkoff was willing to come to either Alicante or Valencia, on Monday morning, to be interviewed and to help the police as much as she could. She preferred Valencia, if there was a choice, so Sofía had agreed on Valencia.

There would have to be a senior officer sitting in at either location, at this point Sofía didn't care. They arranged to meet at Valencia's Joaquín Sorolla station at eleven twenty-five on Monday morning. She promised that, provided Karkoff answered all their questions and gave them time to confirm her information, there was no reason why she shouldn't catch the five-ten and be back in Madrid by ten to seven in the evening. The beauties of the high-speed *Ave* connection!

She put the phone down and went back to mulling over what she knew and what she guessed about the Camilla question. She would need to get it written down in some sort of order before she questioned Karkoff. The designer would be accompanied by her legal team and whilst she had allowed several hours for the interview, follow-up and re-interview, this was her one chance to get some straight answers.

Roberto seemed to be positive that there had been no sign of life at the flat near Lola's, each time he'd checked it. Maybe that was what he'd been doing in the road behind Lola's; the back door to the flat must be there. Perhaps he wasn't as useless as Pedro seemed to think. Was she letting Pedro cloud her judgement with his palpable dislike of the man?

It was all such a mess.

Next step, she would need to talk to Roberto.

Just now though, after yesterday and a sleepless, scared night, she just wanted to go home, hug her family, find some food for the dog and sleep.

Roberto wasn't finding the hospital as easy to navigate as he'd expected. The wards were spread out over two floors and three wings. The room numbers were duplicated on each wing and floor.

He needed to know the missing prefix letter, or he would need to walk each floor. Being in uniform, though, he could make it look like a policeman doing a diligent security sweep, while a patient under threat was being looked after in the hospital.

Chapter 28 – Pamela and Sally's Saturday

Pedro had returned the chips to Pamela, complete with their photos. With copies kept of everything they needed, there was no reason to hang onto the originals.

After he'd gone, Pamela and Sally spent a nostalgic, restful morning looking through the other photos on the chips, sharing memories. Then they chatted about Granny Em and her new boyfriend, giggling over the stories she would probably have when she returned.

The only things that they didn't talk about were the deaths and the attack on Pamela.

Neither wanted to think about any of it today. Pamela was faintly relieved that Pedro was working. Perhaps it was too soon for Sally to have to cope with a new boyfriend when she was still raw from breaking up with Greg. She was still thinking about the break-up when Sally startled her by mentioning Greg's name.

"Sorry, what did you say, Sally?"

"I know, it's so strange! Twice in the last few days, I could have sworn I saw Greg – once near the Charity Shop and once near the Post Office. I caught sight of someone out of the corner of my eye, but each time I turned to look, he wasn't there. Well, why would he be?"

"You know I never met Greg, so what was he like?" Pamela had been dying to ask Sally about her ex, since she'd arrived, upset and exhausted all those months ago, but had been waiting for Sally to raise the subject.

"Well, I was attracted to him by his smile and he is really good-looking. Not in the George Clooney category, but definitely in a Robert Pattinson way," responded Sally smiling sadly, knowing that her mother was now itching to get to the computer to look at photos of the actor.

"It was a long while before I realised that his smile never reached his eyes. It was smooth, practiced and very convincing, but it was never real. The only time I ever saw him take any pleasure was when he hit me. He got 'high' when he was in control, being the centre of everyone's attention. The only way I could ever hurt him back, for the pain he brought me, was by taking his control away from him." She paused, collecting her thoughts.

"I don't think that Granny Em and Aunt Helen ever really believed that Greg was a sociopath, he was always on his best behaviour when they were there. Aunt Helen was actually angry with me, when we broke up. But, I can understand that, I found it hard to admit it to myself – after all, he could be so charming." It was hard for Sally, looking back at how stupid she'd been.

Greg was a master at manipulating her into believing that everyone else was in the wrong and only he had the ability to make her happy, even when she clearly wasn't. She became so deeply unhappy that she began to withdraw from her friends, her work and her family.

Pamela made a movement, as if to stop her from saying more, but Sally shook her head, continuing "No, Mother, I need to tell you. Spending even a little time with Pedro this last few days has made me realise how shallow Greg is, as if I needed any more convincing. Pedro is so much more a man than Greg ever could be. Even if nothing happens with him and it goes nowhere, at least I know, now, that I want someone who cares about me and what I think of things, other than him. I need someone who is interested in what I have to say, not just in silencing me, so that I have to listen to him. As the song goes – I've washed Greg out of my hair. So why am I seeing him all over the place? Should I tell Pedro about him? I'm really glad we have new locks."

They talked through the events that finally made Sally decide to escape to Spain. In the end they decided that Sally's imagination must be running riot. There was nothing for Greg here, so why on earth would he have come?

It was a gruelling session for them both, going over things that had depressed Sally so much that she'd run away, even though she was embracing her decision and her new life.

They would have enjoyed their day even less, had they realised that Greg was sitting less than a hundred metres away. He was enjoying a beer and, surprisingly for him, *Albóndigas de Calabacin,* now he'd discovered that it was a sort of courgette / marrow vegetable with meatballs. He'd been a little mystified when the English translation on the menu had been 'footballs of meat with Zucchini'.

From the moment he'd arrived in Spain his dominant thought was *What on earth did the woman see in this place?* He doubted it was just the sun and having her mother handy. Could it be the food? He couldn't understand why she'd left or how she thought she could hide from him.

Her Aunt Helen was an easy source of information, she'd always liked him. She had even phoned him to tell him how appalled she was that Sally was going to Spain, assuming he knew and that he would want sympathy and support. She'd overheard Sally phoning Pamela to say she was on her way and hadn't booked a return ticket.

Work meant that he couldn't leave straight away. Now, he admitted, it was self-delusion and Helen's reassurances, which convinced him that she'd be back in a few weeks, begging him to take her back. Sally obviously had other ideas.

When people started to notice that she was no longer on his arm at social events and he ran out of excuses, he felt himself becoming more and more angry.

She was embarrassing him.

She was the reason why people at work avoided him.

It was her fault that his flat was no longer clean, tidy and fit for a man of his calibre to live in.

She was the reason for his promotion not going through.

She'd done this deliberately to ruin his life.

She was going to learn that he was not a man to

193

be messed with. She needed to be taught a lesson that she would never forget.

Spain was not the place he'd have chosen, but it had some unexpected advantages. A recent murder case was causing wild speculation and was completely occupying the local bobbies. Whilst he was still furious about how close he'd come to being exposed; he hadn't been seen by anyone who knew him. Although watching Emma waving her new camera around in the Square, the other morning, had been unnerving.

He hadn't used any credit cards since arriving. He'd brought enough cash and stock with him to keep him going for a while. English customs were stupid. They made a great deal of fuss about what people brought into the UK but, apart from the standard and cursory luggage x-rays looking for bombs, they didn't seem to care what was taken out. He'd scattered about twenty vitamin and health supplement pill bottles randomly inside each of the two suitcases he'd brought with him; all claiming slightly different contents. The bottles had been bought from legitimate health food shops, the receipts pushed, with apparent carelessness, into the side pocket of one of the cases.

He might look like a complete hypochondriac, but he really didn't think it was going to be his biggest worry. The crystal meth tablets now inside each resealed container had been dyed a colour roughly matching the original contents.

In case the Spanish customs officers were more awake, he had put four untampered bottles, with their original healthy contents intact, into his cabin luggage, ready to show any officious enquirer.

Always Right

As he'd expected, when he walked through customs in Spain, no one was interested. He'd kept the bottles anyway; with their healthy food supplement contents, they might come in useful. He had no idea how his stomach would react to a foreign diet!

With a street value of around ten euros a tablet and with ninety pills fitting comfortably into each bottle, it had been totally worth it. With no Spanish he'd been a little worried about operating under the radar, it was so much easier in the UK. To his delight, however, he'd had no problem finding needy English-speaking tourists with ready cash in search of an extra holiday thrill, even in sleepy Puerto Amarillo.

Common sense had taken over, though. It would be hard to keep a low profile if he sold too close to where he was staying.

After some thought and a little internet research, he'd taken most of his business an hour down the coast to Benidorm.

If everything worked out well, he thought, ordering another beer from the pretty waitress, he could work out quite a neat retirement plan, here.

He could even open a small health food shop as a cover, there were lots of them about, one more wouldn't be noticed. His UK contacts could supply, and he could set up fake email orders for his extra special 'health supplements', so there was a plausible audit trail for postal deliveries.

He savoured the idea, as he ordered another beer. Spain was working out much better than he'd expected.

Chapter 29 – Room 1104's Saturday

Hospital Room 1104 was receiving a constant stream of visitors with the Saturday rounds of medication changes and doctor visits. It was also opposite the nurse's station, so Roberto, having finally found the right room, had a problem. It would be a good half-hour before the heavy medical presence disappeared and Roberto could act.

The police presence outside Frau Schmeckler's room was sparse. There was only one guard, but he was not someone Roberto knew well.

Alonzo's beat was in the tourist and main holiday beach area of Puerto Amarillo about three miles from the Port area where Roberto now patrolled. Their shifts meant that they'd rarely met, apart from the odd coffee in the station café or the occasional drink in a local bar, on somebody's birthday.

It might be difficult to explain to Alonzo why he was in uniform, today, when he wasn't on duty, so it was just as well he had a change of clothes in his car, even if he had brought them along for his 'get-away' later.

Once he was sure that the policeman was completely engrossed with the pretty nurse on the Ward reception desk and hadn't noticed him, he backed quietly away from his vantage point. When he was clear, he turned, went down the side stairs to the outpatients' area and slipped out of the bustling building.

It took him a few minutes to get back to the car and change into his civvies, without drawing unwanted attention. In that respect, only changing his trousers represented a privacy problem and that was solved when he glared, angrily at the nosy kid who, running ahead of his parents on the way back to their car, had peered in at an awkward moment.

Slightly crumpled, but now in casual clothes, Roberto headed to the hospital's restaurant, where he ordered two coffees and some of today's freshly baked pastries to take away.

Carefully carrying them to the lift, he made his way back to the ward. Once there, he started to walk past Alonzo, as if visiting a room farther down the corridor. As soon he drew level with Room 1104, Alonzo recognised him and greeted him with enthusiasm, pleased to have a fellow officer to talk to.

Roberto offered him one of the coffees and the bag of pastries, saying it would be fine, he wasn't due to visit his sick friend for another hour. He was early, as he'd been worrying about parking, so he could get them another drink and snack, later. Alonzo looked more in need.

Alonzo was quick to admit that he was both hungry and thirsty. They commented that there were no vending machines anywhere near the room he was guarding, and he admitted that he had been watching trolleys of food and hot drinks for patients being wheeled up and down for the last hour.

In fact, he was so thirsty and hungry that he drank both coffees and, in between, ate all the pastries.

Roberto didn't mind, even though he had only laced one of the coffees with the fast-acting laxative he'd picked up from a pharmacy on the way to the hospital; the sweetness of the pastries would disguise the difference in flavours. The more Alonzo drank, the quicker he would need relief.

It took less than fifteen minutes for Alonzo to start hopping from one foot to the other. Roberto, looking concerned, offered to cover guard duty for him. The ward was fairly quiet now, so Alonzo yelled a quick thanks and dashed off towards the toilet.

Roberto's luck was finally changing. Just as he moved towards the seat next to the door of Frau Schmeckler's room, an alarm on the other side of the ward sounded and the nurses at the desk dashed away to deal with whatever the emergency was.

When Roberto let himself into the room, no one in the ward paid any attention to him.

A piece of miscellaneous information picked up at a police forensic lecture he'd attended years ago, made Roberto aware that it took about seven minutes for a healthy person, deprived of oxygen, to die.

Fortunately for him, the Frau was not normally a healthy person. She certainly wasn't right now, nor did she resist, so it took much less than seven minutes for him to complete the job.

When sure she was gone, he took the pillow from her face and replaced it behind her head.

Next, he disconnected the drip and moved her hand, sharply, backwards and forwards a few times so the crumpled bedding would look as if she had moved agitatedly in her sleep, working her drip loose. Once that was done, it took all his strength to shift her onto her side, away from the door. She was amazingly heavy, dead, not to mention floppy. He wriggled her other arm and pulled the bedding as much as he could, positioning her face against the pillow, now trapped against her arm, so that it looked as if she had smothered herself in her sleep.

When he was finally satisfied that it looked like an accident, he went back into the still empty corridor and sat in the guard's chair.

It was another five minutes before Alonzo had recovered enough to resume his seat. He was so grateful for Roberto's help, he didn't think, even for a second, about checking on the patient.

Roberto was miles away, back in the Port, before anyone realised that the Frau was never going to recover.

It would need a coroner, now, to establish the cause and time of death and Roberto would be long gone by then, even assuming that Alonzo thought to mention his dereliction of duty and Roberto's unofficial presence. At least, now, he didn't have to change again before seeing his mother.

Camilla Perez was growing increasingly frustrated. Ever since involving Roberto in her operation, things had been going awry.

She'd been masterminding the whole racket, successfully, for six years, ever since Valentina had passed her over for promotion, for the third time. She didn't need to be told that she was a brilliant seamstress; she knew. After all, it was her designs on which Valentina had built her career.

Valentina had never forgiven her for what she privately called the widow's dress. She had designed, embroidered and finished it, putting it in pride of place on Karkoff's stall when it came to Alicante, six years ago.

She hadn't expected Valentina to attend the event, else she might have waited, but it was the perfect dress to buck the trend …and it had.

It was the volume of orders that the dress attracted at the fair, that was her undoing. She had not entered them onto the books, but word about the new sensation spread. It wasn't long before Karkoff came to see what the buzz in the industry was about; her name was being mentioned in magazine and newspaper reports, alongside a photo of a dress she didn't recognise. The red flag went up for Valentina when the grapevine reported huge sales from which she didn't seem to be benefiting.

It took a lot of fast talking by Camilla to keep her job. She used classic excuses; she was trialling the design, not expecting it to work; she only suggested it was Karkoff's when it became popular and she wanted to surprise her boss.

In the end, though, it was only the Madrid dress designer's business acumen that saved Camilla's job.

To Valentina's fury, the overwhelming demand for the dress eclipsed all her own designs, that year. There were so many orders that, unable to cope on her own, Camilla had been forced to pass on the orders and Valentina could see its popularity. At that point, the dress had been publicly attributed to

Karkoff, so sacking Camilla would have been a bigger embarrassment than keeping her.

Fortunately for Camilla, the dress was not the only innovation she introduced at the Alicante Fair. She also started a lucrative collaboration that had netted her a generous hidden income, until now.

Her health was not up to all the running around that Roberto was making her do.

He really wasn't as bright as she hoped he would be when she'd found him, but he'd been a necessary part of her plan to make a final killing. She had, however, been thinking financially, not literally, and the way he was littering the port with bodies was very disconcerting.

She'd met his father in the last few months of his life, when he was maudlin and wanted nothing more than to spill his woes into a sympathetic ear. She wasn't sure when her genuine sympathy had moved to boredom but, at the point she intended to leave, he had started to share his regrets over his late wife and his policeman son.

His anecdotes were detailed and, when the idea formed in her head, easy to record on her phone. She'd made quite a few notes by time he died.

She'd known him for a few weeks by the time she'd collected enough material, but he hadn't mentioned her to anyone. She'd claimed that she had a brutal husband who would kill them both if he found out.

The ploy had worked.

Getting him to drink himself into a stupor on that last night hadn't been difficult either. Persuading him to walk near the cliff-edge, to see the romantic view from the bar's carpark had been hard, but, luckily, pushing him off the edge had been remarkably easy.

As long as Roberto believed she was his mother, she was safe from him. He hadn't even asked why she'd 'changed' her name, although she had thought of a story about trying to escape her criminal past and his father. Now, though, he was becoming unpredictable and spiralling out of control. She had run out of allies too, and her attempts to stay out of the limelight meant that barely anyone in the port knew she was there.

Her asthma was really slowing her down and her one attempt to remove damning evidence about her activity had been a waste of time. She'd been incredibly lucky that someone else was sneaking about, in the apartment block, at the time she had attacked Señora Wright. She was pretty sure that nobody, besides the cursed boy from next door's restaurant, had seen her in the square. Everyone else had been watching the man running away from the policeman.

A panting, asthmatic, old lady, wobbling her way home was a fairly common sight in a place full of retirees, so she blurred into the background for everyone. The boy though, he had stared straight at her, but then, who would listen to him?

Her fingers were still raw from rushing the dress alterations. Roberto had been too fired up with his revisions to her masterplan to listen. It seemed best to do as he asked. She needed to keep him placated, if the final part of her plan were to work – the one she hadn't shared with him, yet!

Chapter 30 – Saturday Evening

Neither Sofía nor her team were pleased to be called out to the hospital, late on Saturday evening. They were even less pleased when they realised that they had lost a crucial witness.

Sofía requested a forensic team as soon as she heard that Frau Schmeckler was dead and instructed Alonzo to secure the room until they arrived. Fortunately, he had sealed the room, immediately, before ringing his boss, who, in turn, had phoned her, so no time was lost in preserving evidence.

The doctor seemed convinced it was an accidental death, exacerbated by her weakened state, post ricin poisoning. He admitted it was unusual, but pointed out that she was in an 'at-risk' ward because a risk was there, even if it wasn't inevitable. He refused to answer any questions about how a patient, who was supposed to be under constant monitoring could smother themselves.

The more she questioned him, the more irritable and defensive he became. She was fed up and very tired. Finally, she snapped, demanding a full autopsy and a complete forensic examination of the room.

By the time she crawled home and into bed next to her equally exhausted husband, she'd decided that, as soon as they both had time, they would need to review her chosen career.

Well, she thought as she drifted off to sleep, the amount of overtime she had demanded, to get a team to the hospital over the weekend, she might not have much of a career choice left.

It was a worry that Roberto had been to the hospital, even though he'd been gone hours before Frau Schmeckler was found. Alonzo had been keen to relate every detail of his day on duty. He was distraught that he might have missed a murder taking place under his nose. The fact that Alonzo's brief but nasty bout of diarrhoea, occurred when Roberto was conveniently present to cover for him, was worrying; that it happened just after Alonzo ate and drank something given to him by Roberto, was now of real concern.

Was he repeatedly cropping up because he was unlucky? Because he was dirty or was there another, even less palatable reason?

Chapter 31 – Sunday

Pedro wasn't too bothered about working on Sunday. Now that Sally's mother had been involved in whatever was going on, he wanted this case solved as soon as possible.

If Pamela was in danger, so might Sally be. Wherever their relationship was going, whether or not it was developing, he couldn't bear the thought that either might be in danger.

He'd had an early and invigorating run with Cha-Cha before heading into work. It had helped to clear his mind and spending time with his dog was always calming.

He was still furious with Roberto for allowing the CCTV footage from the time of Egnacio's murder to be deleted. He was also more than a little perturbed about the way he had mistreated Lola. There was something basically unstable about the man. Were he not a policeman, Roberto would be very high on his suspect list. But, if he had been the man running from Sally's apartment building, he would have recognised him. However, it had not been Roberto, so everything else had to be an annoying coincidence.

Then there was the business about the wheezing that Pamela had heard, after she was attacked. Clearly, it wasn't the same person he'd chased but it might be a partner. Then he remembered what José said about the old woman who had also been in the square. Odd – he didn't remember seeing her, but his focus was on the running man. Maybe they were in it together.

He decided that he would feel better after checking into the station to enquire about the missing keys. Not that they were needed now, but it was a loose end. It really was an annoying and unnecessary mystery in a sea full of them.

After that, he would head across to Lola's and see if José was about. He needed the boy's help to put together an e-fit of the woman and, with luck, the running man. He'd been closer to both than Pedro had.

Depending on what he discovered and the reports that had come in after Sofía and he finished last night, he'd promised to ring her at home for an update.

It was clear that she also had no love for Roberto's standard of policing, so, unless he wanted to scupper the young policeman's career for good, he would need to be a little careful.

He really liked working with the Guardia, it would be good if he could do more of this. Maybe he should look at the possibility of transferring, he was getting frustrated with the thought of going back to his old duties.

It had been an amazing opportunity to get involved in a murder case as more than a translator. For his opinion to be asked and valued was heady stuff. Being able to show that he was actually contributing towards solving this case would be even better.

Walking into the station, he decided to start the key search by seeing who was on reception duty at the time they were handed in.

To be honest, he was surprised that it hadn't been Roberto on duty but Gonzo had signed in just about the time the paramedic would have been walking up to the desk. Luckily, Gonzo was on duty now, so Pedro walked back to the reception area and waited by the vending machine, sipping something optimistically labelled as coffee, while Gonzo finished with the queue of 'customers' at the desk. When there was a lull and Gonzo had finished writing up everything he needed to record, he was happy to spend some time gossiping with Pedro.

Gonzo knew that Pedro was getting quite a reputation as a go-getter and decided it couldn't hurt to help him on his way up whatever ladder he was climbing. He was therefore pleased, being able to add something to the investigation. He had also seen Pedro with the victim's daughter, Sally, when they'd been walking through the Port, so he wasn't surprised that the attack on Sally's mother was on Pedro's mind.

He described his shift in detail.

He'd arrived and signed in like he always did then, seeing that Roberto was dealing with someone on the desk, he'd nipped to the toilet before going out to the counter. Roberto had left a few minutes later. No, he had no idea about the keys, or who'd handed them in. However, if it helped, he'd found a stray set of keys on the floor near the desk a couple of days later. They'd been put into the station's lost and found box.

As they were on his side of the counter, he'd just assumed that someone from the station must have dropped them.

By the time a very thoughtful Pedro arrived at the café, the Fishermen's Church had emptied its Sunday congregation into the port – much to the appreciation of the local restaurateurs.

Lola's café was as busy as ever, but José wasn't in sight, until Pedro poked his head into the small kitchen.

Surrounded by dirty dishes, the boy needed no second invitation to desert his chores. The other dishwasher, being left to work alone, didn't look as unhappy as Pedro might have expected until José explained. They were on a piece rate and whoever did the most dishes got all the dish-washers' share of the tips.

José didn't mind that much, anything was better than being up to his elbows in suds and, having already been out most of the morning on choir-duty, he wasn't going to win. He never did on a Sunday.

After he'd let his sister know he was being kidnapped, they walked back to the station, chatting.

José was still angry with Roberto.

Even if Lola could be a pain, she was still his sister and no one had any right to hurt her, let alone make her cry.

He confirmed, again, that he often heard footsteps running up the stairs next-door, just after Roberto had left the café, ostensibly to go back to work. He'd never been inside the neighbouring apartment, after all, it wasn't as if they lived at the café and were there all the time to build up relationships with neighbours.

He hadn't even seen the new occupant, so couldn't tell Pedro anything about her except that she wheezed a lot.

He agreed it could be the person he'd seen after the attack on Pamela, especially as he'd heard the wheezing next door on the day that Pamela had been attacked, before the café got busy.

The rasping noise had been louder than usual, through the open window of her flat and barely muffled by the damp of the early evening. He remembered it because the window had slammed shut and, a few minutes later, there had been the muffled sound of a man shouting. Sadly though, he had no idea who it was.

At the station, José not only managed to describe the old woman, he did a very credible job of describing the running man. By the time he'd added his own input, Pedro thought the e-fit picture looked vaguely familiar. Maybe it was some-one he'd seen when he'd been with Sally.

As well as emailing the pictures to Sofía, he sent a copy of each e-fit to his own phone. He would probably need to show them to quite a few people before he got an ID for either of them. Although, there was a strong chance that Valentina Karkoff might identify one of them on Monday, when she met with Sofía.

Still, it would be nice to get the information first.

He'd arranged to meet Sally for a late lunch in a café close to her apartment.

There were a lot of good restaurants nearby, he'd been spoilt for choice and it didn't really matter where they met, it would just be good to spend some time with her, without an audience of his friends or her family.

He was undecided whether to start the conversation off with the pictures or to wait until they'd eaten.

He wrestled with that problem all the way from the station to the restaurant and decided, as he sat down to wait for her, that he had best get it over with first and then they could both relax.

In retrospect, that might have been a mistake.

She arrived smiling and happy and they both started to talk at the same time. She was apologising for being late and he for needing to discuss business and the attack on her mother.

Sally was quite understanding and agreed to see both the photos. She didn't expect to recognise either.

The old woman, as expected, was a complete stranger to her. She could have been one of the women in the café, but she didn't think so. Next, he flicked to the e-fit of the man.

Sally went white.

Pedro was aghast, the bubbly happy Sally that he was falling in love with seemed to shrivel as she stared at the picture. She looked completely distraught and, to his horror, burst into tears.

Lunch was over before it had even started.

He cancelled their order and asked for two cups of the hot sweet chocolate, that all Spanish bars seemed to stock, to be brought to the table. She didn't speak until she'd taken a sip of the comfortingly syrupy drink.

"I'm so sorry, Pedro, you must think I'm mad" was all she could say.

He answered that it was obvious that she knew the man. Could he be the person who attacked her mother? Could he be the killer?

"No, I don't think so, he never even met my mother and he'd never been to Spain, when I knew him. It is my ex-fiancé, Greg. I am mainly here because I ran away from him. I was saying to mother, yesterday, that I'd had the strange feeling that I'd seen him in the Port, but I convinced myself that I was wrong. It doesn't make sense. Why would he be here? How could he know where I am? But, out of all the places in Spain, why else would he have chosen to come to the port?" She paused for a few minutes and then added, "Maybe my Aunt Helen or my Gran told him, I don't think either of them have any real idea what he's like or even why we broke up."

Haltingly, she told him what she'd finally managed to tell her mother only the day before. Having forced herself to stay silent for so many months, it was cathartic to tell her story twice in as many days, but she was afraid of what Pedro would think of her now.

She needn't have worried; of all the people she could ever tell, a policeman was one of the few to understand the maxim that 'victims aren't responsible for the crime'. He also understood that, in the case of abuse, the victim was often bullied and browbeaten into thinking that the attacks on them were justified.

They left the café and he walked her down to the

seafront and along the beach, towards a small bay he knew, off the tourist track.

The quietness and sound of the lapping waves were soothing. The warm sunshine and the salty ozone scent of the sea were healing.

They stopped to sit on a rock and after a few minutes, soaking up the calm, everything spilled out of her.

Now that she knew she wasn't going mad and really had been seeing Greg in the port, she was able to give Pedro the locations and approximate times she'd seen him.

It didn't take Pedro long to realise that whatever Greg was, he couldn't be their killer.

He would deal with Greg later.

Right now, he had to get Sally home to her mother, check they were both safe and find out who the old woman was. However unlikely it was, it looked as if their chief suspect for the attack on Pamela was an asthmatic pensioner.

He walked Sally back to the flat, but, at her request, didn't go in with her. He felt bad leaving, but it was understandable that she wanted to be alone with her mother right now.

Five hundred kilometres away, sipping wine with Miguel, in a bodega on the outskirts of Jaén, Emma was happier than she'd been in as long as she could remember. The spotty phone reception up in the Andalusian mountains hadn't worried her unduly. After all, what emergencies were Sally and Pamela likely to be having?

Helen didn't speak to her as much as she used to,

since they'd rowed about Sally's break-up with Greg, so it was extremely unlikely that she was missing any important news.

Thinking of Helen reminded her of their last 'discussion'. Helen had wanted to include an invitation to Greg for a restaurant meal they were planning with old friends.

Emma had flatly refused.

When Helen had insisted, saying that Greg was hoping to get back with Sally, so should go as 'part of the family' Emma just cancelled her seat at the table and had stayed home. She didn't want to row with her daughter in public and hadn't wanted to see Greg again.

Goodness knows what they'd talked about, in her absence but, at a guess, her ears should have been burning. Presumably, dinner went well. Who knew? Helen hadn't been in touch since, but it had sparked Emma's decision to check up on Pamela and Sally.

Once reassured that Sally was happy with her new life, she hadn't needed to hover and, anyway, she still had a couple of weeks left, to spend with Sally, before needing to be back in the UK. That was, if she decided to go back...

She couldn't pin down why she'd been relieved when Sally left Greg, but she was. There was something about him that made her hackles rise.

She had been as non-committal as possible when Sally first brought him to see her, but there was something in his eyes and a fleeting expression that occasionally flickered across his face that made her uncomfortable.

Greg reminded her of an actor she'd met when

she was about Sally's age – a complete narcissist.

Greg had all the right words, said everything just as he should, when he should, but she'd seen far less warmth in his eyes in all the time he had spent with them than she'd seen in Pedro's eyes in the first few minutes after meeting him.

She didn't fully understand why Sally had abandoned her job and come to Spain, instead of just showing Greg the door, but perhaps Pamela needed her daughter, she had suffered such a traumatic few years – hadn't they both?

Unlike Emma's problems, Pamela's hadn't ended with Mark's death. Discovering the cancer so soon after being widowed must have been awful.

Yes, having lost a father and ended a relationship with Greg, maybe Sally missed her mother as much as her mother missed her.

The more Emma thought about it, she clearer she believed that they both needed her now more than Helen did.

Maybe she should start looking for a small place to stay, when she and Miguel finally decided to return to Puerto Amarillo.

It would be nice to see more of Miguel, too.

After the last few days, the thought of going back to her drab little English cottage was losing its appeal.

Would Helen miss her, if she stayed?

Probably not.

Now that Helen's children were getting older, her babysitting duties had reduced a lot. She really wasn't cut-out to be a chauffeur and the school-runs weren't as easy as they had been when the children were little.

She was getting tired of being expected to be on hand, all the time, to run around after them.

Sometimes she found Helen's excuses for not being much of a parent were a little hollow. She loved her daughter, her only remaining child, but maybe it was time to give Helen some space. Helen needed to be the one spending time with her children, otherwise, one day, she might have to face the regrets that Emma lived with, every day.

She should have spent more time with Mark.

Now she would like to make up for that by spending more time with Sally.

Miguel wanted her to stay in Spain, too. He'd offered her a home and she knew his children and their families would be pleased; she had known them all since they were born. For years they had been close enough for her to continue to send cards and the odd present after her return to the UK. Exchanging emails and letters had also been an opportunity for her to help them in their English studies and it had been good to have a link to the past. She thought maybe baby-steps first, though. Somewhere of her own, a small rented flat would do, at least until she and Miguel had spent a bit more time together. She was comfortable with him, and could be happy, too. It wasn't what she'd had with Frank. Nothing could be the same but being with Miguel felt right. She really felt that Marta would approve, and Frank would have understood.

She would also have the chance to see more of Sally, without being intrusive.

She could still see Helen, every few months, in the same way that she'd dumped herself on Pamela and

Sally. Helen had enough space to put her up occasionally.

In between visits, she could learn how to use Skype and all the other messaging apps her grandchildren had told her she should be using.

Following that thought, she must recharge her phone on their next stop. She'd let the battery go flat when they'd had no reception. She'd read somewhere that it was healthy to let a phone battery run down, between charges. Something about extending the battery life. Though, truth be told, she had simply forgotten it, when it stopped getting a signal!

She knew that Miguel was still waiting for an answer to the question he'd asked last night. Emma decided that she now knew the answer.

Closing the hotel's door behind her, she turned to embrace the day's warmth. After taking a deep breath, she walked towards Miguel and into the sunshine – a metaphor that was not lost on her, as she took his arm and they walked along the street together, admiring the shops, the people and everything in-between.

Chapter 32 – Sunday Evening

Sofía was exhausted. Leading an investigation this complex, with so many different leads and angles was tougher than she expected. She felt she was rising to the challenge, but had to hope that not every case, where she was the lead, would be this hard.

She'd spent a lot of time on the phone since Pedro had eliminated Greg from the attack. It was a relief to have got rid of the red herring, even if it was clear that the man was up to something, it was not connected with the case she was most concerned about. It was a problem for another day.

It had taken a great deal of shouting to unblock the stalled search warrant she'd requested, days ago, for Karkoff's apartment in the port. It turned out that the powers that be wanted her to interview the designer before they would allow the premises to be disturbed. Karkoff clearly had some seriously powerful contacts. They caved in when she'd threatened to take Valentina's interview in the police station, instead of trailing up to Valencia, as a courtesy. It was within her rights as the investigating officer and they knew it.

The only stipulation to the warrant was that Sofía be present.

Head Office had been so clever – they'd let her win the battle, but only on condition that she lost the war. The only ways she could be present at the search of the studio were, firstly – if she didn't interview Karkoff on Monday – and it was imperative that she did – or, secondly, if she waited until after the interview. So, they'd won, she had to interview the designer first.

However, she would be heading straight to the port, as soon as she left the interview. There could be no more delays.

To make absolutely sure that she had all the paperwork with her, she got head office to fax the warrants to her home. It was too late to tell anyone at the local station that she had them, but maybe that was a good thing.

As far as everyone else was concerned, the petition to enter the apartment next to Lola's café was still waiting to be approved. Perhaps that was the way she would leave it, for now. Everything inside her screamed that it was important that the occupants continued to think they were safe.

There was a strong possibility that, if Roberto found out about the warrant being approved, the flat would be empty and its residents long gone by the time she returned on Monday evening. The question would then be – would they have left because Roberto jumped the gun and his enthusiasm tipped them off, or because Roberto was involved? Sadly, the incident at the hospital and what Pedro had told her about Pamela's apartment keys, the latter was the most likely scenario. It was better to avoid alerting anyone.

It was a very quiet Sofía who joined her husband and baby for their evening meal. Fritzy had made himself completely at home and absolutely refused to give up his place on the settee, when they finally settled down.

With Rosa fast asleep in her daybed, beside them, Sofía snuggled between her husband and the dog and finally relaxed.

Chapter 33 – Sofía's Monday

Valencia's Joaquín Sorolla Railway Station was always busy, but the city police had managed to sequester a small waiting room, near the platform where the Madrid train was due to arrive.

Sofía had made sure that the Valencian police had photos of the designer and knew her seat number so they would be ready to escort Valentina and her team to the interview, as soon as she exited the train. They didn't have time to mess about.

She'd printed off a list of the most important questions that needed answers and had made notes about peripheral questions. Her shoulder bag was bulging with papers and printed photos, not helped by the tablet that was also in it, with its charger.

Sofía was weary, it had been a long gruelling week since Egnacio's body was found, with many twists and turns.

Whilst sure that Valentina Karkoff was not guilty of the murder and unlikely to have all the answers, Sofía couldn't be sure that she was innocent of an earlier crime that created the motive for everything else that followed.

Carefully taking everything out of her bag and placing it on the table, she settled at the interview table.

She checked that she had all Pamela's photos on her tablet as well as the official ones for the case, before she tidied the papers into neat piles and waited for the train. The station café had provided decent coffee and enough cups, for whatever size army of lawyers accompanied Valentina.

Placing the paperwork in the order she needed, reminded her of the first time she had interviewed a suspect away from the office, like this. Knowing that they were bringing along some high-powered legal weight, she had slipped each piece of information into shiny, new, plastic bags, sorted by topic. It had looked superbly efficient, until she started to lift them out of her case. The bags were so new, so shiny and smooth that they and their contents started to slip and slither as soon as she put them down.

The more she grabbed at them, the more their contents spilled. The more she panicked and grabbed, the greater the muddle.

At the worst possible moment, whilst retrieving paperwork from the floor, the suspect and accompanying legal team had been ushered into the room and for the rest of the interview, she'd been in a panic, having to dive through all the slippery and sliding documents to search for the info she needed for every question. Afterwards, as soon as she'd calmed down, she'd taken great pleasure in visiting a *punte verde* and pushing every new, shiny, plastic wallet into a plastic recycling bin. At least she'd been asking and not answering questions but, even so, it could not have been a bigger disaster.

This time and every time since, for any meeting, let alone an interview, she arrived early enough to avoid unfortunate issues.

Just as well this time, she thought, as the tannoy announced that the Madrid train was early. The only bright spot was that her boss was too busy to come, so other than the Valencian policeman who'd escorted Ms Karkoff from the train, she was on her own.

Valentina had brought three other people with her but only one of them was a lawyer. The second companion introduced himself as an accountant, the other was an athletic-looking woman, tall, slim and someone who clearly should be a model, if she wasn't one already.

She was.

After a brief round of introductions, before Sofía and her colleague from Valencia could start the interview, Karkoff's solicitor took over the meeting.

Clearing his throat and gesturing everyone to sit, he began. "My client, Señora Karkoff has a statement that she wants me to read out, before you address any questions to her. Then, and only then, is she prepared to answer any questions that you may have for her.

I, Valentina Karkoff, make this statement of my own volition and free will.

I have been aware for some time that Camilla Perez, one of my designers, has been cheating me. She is exceptionally skilful as a seamstress and has been responsible for some of my best-selling lines, but she is a chronic liar and has been stealing from me for years.

Until a few months ago, it has always been

small amounts, that I have been prepared to overlook for the income that she brings me.

This year, however, she has excelled herself.

The studio in Puerto Amarillo that has been advertised as one of my new ventures, isn't.

It is my intention to open branches in Barcelona, Valencia and Malaga, but I would never have considered Puerto Amarillo as a suitable location ...nor ever have put Camilla in charge of such a venture.

Camilla is still on my payroll for the next few days, but only because she is on notice. Actually, she left my employ three months ago when I discovered that she was ordering equipment, material and jewellery, for her own use, from my suppliers and that these were being delivered to a place I knew nothing about.

I am still trying to assess the full extent of the damage done to my business and reputation.

I am in the process of making a denuncia against her.

I have been very busy trying to minimise the damage her actions have done to my business, so I extend my apologies to the Guardia for not having made myself available sooner. I wish to co-operate with the police investigation as much as possible and, providing my accountant and solicitor are present, I am happy to make my account books available to the police in Madrid, if that will help you to uncover the extent of her involvement in any crime she may have committed, without my knowledge."

All the time the solicitor read from the statement, he kept glancing sideways at Valentina and Sofía, as if to gauge their reaction.

Sofía's attention had been completely focussed on Valentina's face, so it took her a few minutes to run through her notes and tick the points that the statement covered. Finally, she looked up and spoke.

"Thank you for your co-operation, I take it that your accountant and solicitor will be accompanying me back to Puerto Amarillo, for the benefit of our forensic accountants?"

"Yes, my lawyer advised that they should both accompany me, for that purpose."

"...And the senora, your model? She has attended the meeting because?"

Valentina raised her hand to stop Sofía, so she could answer, "I brought Julia because she too should go back with you to your Port, she has worked more closely with Camilla than I have. She started with me just before the Alicante Fair you mentioned in your messages – she went there with Camilla, to model some of the pieces. We thought this would be gesture of goodwill from me, to show that I am co-operating. I also think that Julia will be able to tell you more about Camilla than I can."

Sofía was not thrilled at the thought of cramming three people into her small car, not least as it would mean five minutes untangling the baby seat she'd only just reinstalled, yesterday, and cleaning Sunday's baby biscuit crumbs and toys from the back seats.

Still, it was only one day's worth of baby mess.

At least the non-baby part of the car was still

immaculate from its recent deep-clean and she was pleased at Karkoff's initiative.

It could be a big help.

She would need to ditch them somewhere, before heading to the flat, though. Perhaps, she could take them to Lola's, then after the search, take Julia up to the studio to look around and see what should and shouldn't be there for a legitimate designer.

The rest of the interview was routine. Valentina confirmed that it *was* Camilla on the stall, in Pamela's pictures, but didn't recognise anyone else in any of the photos. Julia seemed very interested in a couple of the shots, but agreed to chat after Valentina was finished, rather than delay her.

The only surprise was the information Valentina supplied about the source of the jewellery she used, to adorn and accessorise the pieces she sold. Most of the jewellery was costume jewellery, made as bespoke pieces in the Salamanca District of Madrid. "For the clients who want the best available, I work with some of the top *Calle de Serrano* designers, so the pieces I design are complimented and precisely matched by the jewellery. I do not like baubles sewn into my pieces, I design for elegant women, not Christmas trees!"

Sofía took this moment to show Karkoff a photo of the dress worn by Pamela's young sitter. It was clear, from the expression on Valentina's face, that she was not happy.

"Has this been advertised as one of my designs?" she demanded. Anger spilled from her, when Sofía nodded, "Pablo, Boris, when you get to the Port, you need to see what damage Camilla has done with this little venture of hers. I will not be held responsible for work as poor as this!"

It was clear from the way that Pablo, the solicitor, and Boris, the accountant, exchanged glances, that they had experienced Valentina's wrath before.

In the foreground of the photo of the dress, on the mannequin, was the out of focus edge of the painting. Valentina took this in and looked horrified, "will that dress be immortalised in oils? Is nothing sacred? Show me the painting now!"

Sofía saw no harm in showing off Pamela's prowess as an artist, so flicked through the tablet and showed the designer some stills she had taken of the portrait and the jewellery details.

"Impressive," Karkoff decided, "the dress is dreadful, but the painting is superb. Does the painter live in your Puerto, in the provinces? Your locals, they can afford this quality of artist?" She paused, then answered her own question, "Clearly they can..."

Looking pointedly at her watch, she added "Maybe I should have her visit my studio in Madrid, once this is over, I might have some work for her. Do give her my card."

Before she left, alone, to catch her train back to Madrid, Valentina spoke briefly to Boris, in Russian.

Once she'd gone, Sofía showed her passengers where to wait for her, on the opposite side of the road from the taxi-rank, outside the station. Then, while Julia, Pablo and Boris walked slowly out of the station, she dashed to the carpark, threw everything, including the baby-seat and her notes, into the boot and, after settling the ransom for the car, at the machine next to the exit, drove round the station, to pick up her 'guests'.

During the drive back to Puerto Amarillo, Julia sat in the front passenger seat and phoned a couple of hotels, having looked up the numbers on her phone, from a list of places recommended by Sofía. She managed to book the three of them into the same hotel.

It was unusual for a decent hotel to have vacancies at this time of year – a result of the murders no doubt.

Boris and Pablo, in the back, were silent.

Julia, however, was not, she chatted freely about 'the ghastly Camilla'. It was obvious that she didn't like her!

As they cruised south along the A7 'Mediterranean Motorway', Julia regaled Sofía with various anecdotes about how Camilla had not designed anything good since her 'Black Widow' fluke. As Julia was the heroine of every tale, Sofía was inclined to dismiss all but a few useful snippets of information.

It was clear that Camilla had felt under-appreciated and was bitter. When she'd suddenly announced that she had a long-lost son and wanted time off to spend with him, it had coincided with a Karkoff tantrum and she'd been given notice.

At this point the lawyer interjected and warned Julia to tell no more stories about her boss.

The rest of the trip was very quiet.

Michaela Orme

Chapter 34 – Monday Evening

Roberto was angry...

No, he was beyond angry!

His Saturday had been spent sorting out the Frau and other loose ends. His Sunday was filled, trying to sort out his mother's mess. His Monday was all but lost being interviewed by Pedro, of all people, and now his mother wasn't taking his calls.

It was clear that his career in the police force was nearing its end. Pedro obviously suspected him of some sort of involvement in the hospital death. He only had until the completion of the full autopsy on the Frau, to get everything sorted: to get the money and his mother and run. He didn't mind abandoning his old car, but he was sad about leaving the motor bike. Still, he would have more than enough money for a new one!

His mother held the key and had the stash. It was she who'd rigged the dresses and had the contacts to enable them to liquidate their assets.

He needed her.

The thought occurred to him, after the ninth failed call, that apart from being her son, she didn't really need him, anymore.

A car reversed out from a small side road, in front of him, missing him by inches as he swerved to avoid being hit. The driver was clearly a motorbike blind

228

tourist – *un estúpido*. Another day it would have been a pleasure to have booked him and hauled him off to the station. Today he was too busy. He revved the engine, angrily, as he accelerated away and headed his bike towards the port.

Sofía was tired after dropping off the three members of Karkoff's firm. She'd decided against involving them in any way with the visit to the studio, so she drove them to their hotel, where their rooms overlooked the port. In a few minutes, they would have a good view of the proceedings on the other side of the bay if they looked out of their windows.

Pedro had rung her about Sally's boyfriend matching the e-fit picture he'd emailed her, so she wasn't entirely surprised to see the e-fit man sitting in the hotel's bar, as she passed by. She would let Sally know where he was staying later, the mystery of why he was running from the apartment block after the attack on Pamela, was one for another day. He might even end up as a witness, who knows what he'd seen.

When she'd stopped for petrol, about half an hour north of the port, leaving the passengers in the car, she had rung head office to arrange to meet with the Guardia team outside the back of Lola's restaurant. She still had about ten minutes to get there. She'd suggested, as a courtesy, that Pedro be invited to attend as a representative of the local force. He had been an incredibly useful resource. If he couldn't be persuaded to transfer to the Guardia, she would definitely recommend that he be the main local liaison for any future investigations in the area.

By the time she arrived, the forensic team was already suited and booted in the coveralls required to keep the flat uncontaminated, should there be any indication that it was, as she suspected, a crime scene. The SWAT team was ready and equipped with a Halligan Bar to force entry into the flat, if there was no answer or if the landlord failed to show up with the keys.

She'd noticed Roberto's motorbike parked near the entrance to Lola's kitchen when she arrived. She wasn't happy that he was anywhere near, but maybe he was visiting his girlfriend.

A few minutes after her arrival, the landlord drove up and parked a few yards down from the police van. He met them at the door, formally handing her the keys he had been ordered to give her, then left, as instructed by the young officer who had not let him out of his sight or hearing since presenting the warrant.

Finally, they were inside the apartment.

Steps ran up inside the small bare entrance hall. There was nothing to look at downstairs, so they moved straight up to the main apartment.

The flat was not laid out as they might have expected a fashion business to be. There was a small reception cum waiting area and a second room, clearly used as a workshop, with good lighting, a cutting table and a sewing machine – but there was only just enough room for one worker. It was never going to be big enough for a high-status design studio, even if one of the two small bedrooms was used as an office.

In the only bathroom, the toilet seat was up and the rim and floor were stained with urine. The bowl was unflushed, and the yellowing urine on the floor uncongealed, despite the heat, although it was beginning to thicken and smell.

As the rest of the bathroom was quite clean, it seemed incongruous. Flies were beginning to be attracted to the viscous liquid so, as soon as photos had been taken of the room, the windows were closed, the door shut and the room left as they'd found it.

There was barely enough room for a single bed in the cluttered smaller bedroom, though it showed plenty evidence of use – from the stubbed cigarettes in the ashtray, to the S and M porn mags near the bed and the clothes in the wardrobe.

A cursory look showed that there was a pressed and clean police uniform conspicuously incongruous amongst the jeans and t-shirts: a local police uniform. That, and the motor-bike and car keys thrown casually on the bedside table, told Sofía and Pedro that their worst suspicions were correct. Roberto must spend time here.

The second bedroom was larger and bare of ornaments and personality. The large double bed was stripped and the drawers and wardrobe empty, as was the rest of the room, apart from a couple of suitcases, standing ready by the door into the hall.

On top of the larger case was a travel wallet from a local travel agent. Inside it was a single airline ticket in the name of Camilla Perez.

As they moved back into the hall, the Guardia Tech, outside the closed kitchen door signalled that he had a problem. "The door is blocked by something heavy, there could be someone in there." Sofía nodded in acknowledgement and radioed the two-man team standing by at the bottom of the fire-escape, to prevent anyone leaving the apartment through the kitchen.

Silently, the two officers climbed the steps that led up behind the flat. At the top, they peered cautiously in through the window. "First Sergeant, there are two bodies on the floor. A man has fallen against the back door, we can only just see the feet of a woman, but she may be what is blocking the inside door. Neither are showing any sign of movement. There is a lot of fresh blood, we need the Forensics team to photograph this before we enter – you might be better accessing the kitchen, from where you are."

Chapter 35 – A Saturday Wedding

It had taken most of the week to get the the forensic test results back from the bodies in the kitchen, Marianne and Frau Schmeckler.

There had been no rush, except the need to sign the case off. It was clear that murders were solved.

Fortunately, Sofía had filed her suspicions and her outline of the case before going to the flat. They had, after all been part of her reasoning when she finally got her warrant.

As a result, the fact that the perpetrators were both dead was a bonus to her cynical, politically aware boss – a neat satisfying ending that would not cost them months in court and therefore looked good in the press. Tourists could resume their holidays with the thrill of having been close to a notorious series of murders, without fearing that a murderer still lurked.

Even though the case was pretty much over, there were still some loose ends to tidy up.

The lawyer and accountant from Valentina Karkoff had been extremely helpful, signposting the discrepancies in Camilla's accounting and how she had skimmed money from Karkoff's clients.

She had repeatedly over-ordered material and bumped the price of the garments to include a 'second' outfit, whilst only submitting the sale of one garment at its original price to the accounts.

Here, the scam had been a lot more sophisticated, but had involved too many people. Disentangling it all took days of interviews and to-ing and fro-ing.

She was glad to be able to give Pedro the final debrief, along with permission to release the information where he saw fit, and the offer of a job in her new department.

Yes, her bosses were very happy with her. She would be working directly with ports up and down the coast and was to be given a base office at the Policía Local Office in Puerto Amarillo.

She was getting an acting promotion to *Brigada* and permission to pick her own team from the officers in her section and, after she asked, local police. With Pedro and some of her own well-honed team, she had high hopes for some very successful investigations.

Her husband was also pleased as it would cut her travel time down, significantly, and, if he was to babysit a small dachshund as well as their daughter, Sofía needed to be home for at least some of the walking and pooper-scooping!

Pedro was flattered and not a little excited at the thought of moving to the Guardia, but he now had someone important to discuss it with first, and she had been very busy all week organising the wedding, as was he.

He decided to wait until after the ceremony to update Sally and Pamela on the final dregs of the investigation.

Emma had spent all week, since she got back, buying an outfit for the ceremony and looking for a flat in the port.

Sally and Pamela were thrilled at the thought of her coming to live there and relieved that it had not been she who'd told Greg where Sally had gone.

Helen had admitted, over the phone to her mother, that Sally's move to Spain might have come up as a topic of conversation when Greg had been at the dinner. Helen was impossible! It was her daughter's complete thoughtlessness and insensitivity that had influenced Emma's final decision to stay in Spain.

Emma still had her legal documentation and NIE (National Identity Number) from when she had lived there, as she'd left all the paperwork in Spain with Pamela. It was buried deep in Sally's filing cabinet, in her office, with the family's wills and old passports, but it didn't take long to find, as it was in the only drawer that Sally hadn't sorted through since commandeering the office from her mother.

Armed with her Spanish ID and her passports, opening a new bank account at Emma's old branch wasn't difficult. Transferring money from the UK wasn't too hard from the Spanish end, either, as she was able to use the same currency company she'd used when they'd sold up. Her only difficulty was convincing her UK account manager that she really wanted to move that much money to the currency broker, without her visiting a branch in person. It was clear they were convinced she was being held for ransom and having seen a few estate agency listings, the thought crossed her mind that they might be right.

It wasn't really funny though.

Dealing with her UK bank from abroad was fraught, to say the least.

First, they blocked her from moving more than ten thousand pounds a day out of her account, over the internet. They said, when she phoned, that this was standard policy, to stop money-laundering, which was ironic as they'd raised no questions when she moved the money from the house sale in Spain into the UK account a few years earlier. Then, after a couple of days, they froze her account and forced her to go through a full fraud check over the telephone.

They seemed convinced that, because of her age, she must be under coercion, being scammed or feeble-minded. Her slight deafness, over the phone, added nothing to help her because, when they heard Sally, repeating what they were saying loud enough for Emma to hear, when the call on speaker was muffled, they shut the call down and insisted that they call Emma back and that she be completely alone when she talked to them! She got quite stroppy, in the end, telling them that, if she had to be on her own, they would have to speak a lot slower and more clearly, on a better line! Eventually, she was able to convince them that she fully understood the risks of them relinquishing their control over her money and enough was transferred to give her some options. So, all that was left to do was find a place to live and leave Pamela in peace.

The organising for the wedding, was remarkably complicated even though it was a civil ceremony, so Sally had little time to worry about the murders, except for that first night.

After Pedro phoned her and told her about Roberto's death and apparent involvement, she'd rushed down to see Lola, to make sure that she was alright.

She'd found Lola in shock, but also a little relieved. Frightened of Roberto's mood swings and more than a little worried about how her brother reacted to him Lola had started to be frightened. She had seen slow embers burning that could have developed into a nasty, violent fire, with José caught in its heart.

Roberto's death doused the flames.

Sally hadn't been able to spend much time with Pedro, since the discovery of the bodies, as Grandma Emma took up quite a bit of her week, not only with the battle with the bank, but also being dragged round shops and estate agencies. Then there was the chauffeuring to restaurants, where Emma regaled her friends with stories about her adventures with Miguel, down south. To be fair though, it did sound awfully romantic to Sally.

Now Saturday was here, and it was time to get to the registry office.

The wedding was superb. The Mayor had agreed to officiate and although it was not a huge event, the two grooms made a splendid splash of colour.

Following Raoul's wistful idea of grey garbed guests, Sally had given all those attending strict instructions to stick to grey and white. Raoul and Carlos wore smart, tailored, deep-purple suits with pale mauve shirts and pearl-grey ties – nothing too flamboyant, all very tasteful, but as the only colour in the room they became the rightful focus of every photograph.

It was amazing how many shades of grey there were, thought Sally as she watched the happy couple enjoy the wedding reception that Pedro had organised at a local beach-restaurant. From shimmering pearly pink greys to the smart sombre charcoal grey of the mayor's suit, no one had quite managed 'drab'.

Pedro joined her and they finally relaxed. Sitting comfortably close to her, he whispered his regret that he still had to do the 'reveal' for Emma, the grooms and Pamela. Maybe after the wedding had not been his best idea.

Sally smiled, if this relationship developed, they would have many more evenings to enjoy after this one, so she could wait.

Chapter 36 – The Story Begins

As the reception started to warm-up and the evening started to cool down, the six of them slipped into a side room with a couple of bottles of wine and Pedro who brought everyone up to date.

"As you know," he began, without delay, "Camilla Perez rented the apartment above the jeweller and pretended it was a branch of Karkoff's empire. Cashing in on Valentina's reputation and existing orders from this area, like the Garcia's, was crucial to the scheme, as it brought her rich clients with clout. She chose Puerto Amarillo months ago, because she already had a regular arrangement with Frau Schmeckler and Egnacio. Marianne was only involved because she was the Frau's partner and book-keeper. The Frau was light-fingered and liked to travel. She was an unlikely and therefore successful thief."

Once his audience contained their astonishment Pedro continued with his next revelation. "Egnacio was, essentially, a fence for smuggled gems, taking them off their mounts and resetting them into either antique silver and gold pieces that had stones missing, or designing jewellery for them. Camilla was the brains and the enabler."

Turning to Pamela, he said, "What you and your husband photographed in Alicante, was their annual stockholder's meeting, where they would discuss the previous year's profits, distribute the takings and line up targets." Addressing them all again, Pedro continued.

"Camilla would case the houses of the rich clients who employed Karkoff. She was an excellent craftswoman and seamstress, but according to Julia, Karkoff's model, not much of a designer. It's likely that she copied her Widow's dress from a junior designer who worked with her, but who went missing shortly before the Fair. It was assumed that the young designer had gone back to the provinces after breaking up with her boyfriend, so she wasn't reported missing until several weeks after the fair and the link to Camilla was not made. In the last week, however, we've found other similar designs in Camilla's portfolio case that had the young designer's initials on them. We also found sketches of jewellery supposedly done to make sure they enhanced Karkoff's dresses – but almost certainly done to find buyers who would never know the gems they selected were effectively stolen to their order and repurposed."

Pausing only to sip his drink, he could tell that they were all eager to hear the rest of the story, so went on, quickly.

"This year, however, was to be the last big kill. As it turned out – literally! Camilla was getting too breathless and wheezy to continue with the sham, the constant travelling was getting too much for her, especially as her relationship with her employer was on the rocks. The Frau was reaching the end of her stealing-to-order career, she wanted to retire.

So, Camilla needed a way out.

For her new plan, she needed to be based on the coast with easy, close access to a large passenger and freight port like Alicante or, even better, Valencia. Already having contacts in Puerto Amarillo, including a fence for the jewellery, she made arrangements to come to the port. It was perfect, a halfway point between the two big Costa Blanca ports. She then used contacts she'd made in the past, visiting Columbia, Venezuela and Brazil, under the cover of working on Karkoff's South American shows, to buy blood diamonds. She got them cut in situ and then smuggled them into Spain jumbled alongside costume jewellery pieces that were mounted, ready to be sewn onto material. They would have looked ready for immediate insertion into Karkoff's dresses. Innocently assisted by Señor Garcia, she brought them into the port and sent both the real and fake gems to Egnacio, for him to separate."

All in his audience were obviously impatient when Pedro stopped to wet his lips again, so he went on quickly.

"While she'd been researching the criminal network, knowing that she needed to shift a fortune in diamonds, she met Roberto's father. From him, she discovered that Roberto was a very unhappy and frustrated policeman. She saw, in the lost young man with a violent streak, the perfect strong-arm partner she needed to cut out the Frau and Marianne. We don't think she intended to kill Egnacio, but everything unravelled because of a mistake. The brooch that Herbert found in the Frau's kitchen had eleven fake diamonds mounted on it. Egnacio's failing eyesight and his miserly way with lighting, resulted in him accidentally handing Camilla eleven high-carat diamonds to mount and sew into Senorita Garcia's dress. He then mistakenly used the fakes in the brooch. We don't think she noticed because she was not the expert on gems – that was the Frau and Egnacio's area of expertise."

Everyone gasped, realising the enormity of Egnacio's mistake and Pedro nodded, "Yes, when Frau Schmeckler saw the brooch that she'd ordered for a rich client, she was more than a little dismayed.

Assuming that Egnacio was trying to swindle his partners, she went straight to Camilla to confer. By then, the dress with the real diamonds was sitting in Pamela's studio and the fake and therefore valueless brooch had mysteriously disappeared from where the Frau had hurriedly popped it, out of the cleaner's way, on top of the fridge. Camilla must have decided it was an opportunity to lose the Frau and Marianne in one fell swoop. Her problem was that the 'twin dress' only had nine fake stones, all she'd had left in that size. While she was mulling the problem over, we have records that show she had a call from Egnacio, probably confessing the mistake and telling her that Herbert had brought the brooch with the fake stones back."

Now that Pedro was discussing the murders, his listeners were literally on the edge of their seats!

"We know that Roberto went to the jeweller's shop to take care of Egnacio. If Camilla sent him, it was a massive mistake. Roberto was volatile and Egnacio greedy, so it is possible that the jeweller demanded a refund of the hundred euros he'd paid out to Herbert or found something else to argue about with Roberto. However it happened, Roberto must have lost his temper completely and grabbed the first weapon he saw. The problem of using such a fragile antique blade was its lack of smooth edges and the small nicks and abrasions on the blade. The forensic team found traces of Roberto's DNA on tiny particles of skin from the blade and handle of the Kris."

Pedro then continued by describing what the police suspected – that they believed that, knowing it was worthless, Roberto must have left the brooch there.

Meanwhile, Frau Schmeckler, knowing nothing about Roberto's involvement, had sent Marianne and Camilla to the jeweller.

Marianne could not have expected to find a dead body when she entered the shop to retrieve the fake brooch. However, Camilla did know, from Roberto, what they would find, so probably waited at the café – to make sure Marianne was the first on the scene. She probably expected her to take the brooch, which now included traces of Egnacio's blood in its decoration. Perhaps she hoped it could be used to frame Marianne or the Frau, but that plan was spoiled when Marianne came out of the shop without it and worse, without drawing anyone's attention to having been inside. Camilla's initial attempt to frame one of her partners was clearly thwarted, so she had to find an excuse to wait at the café to see what developed.

"Marianne's fingerprints were on Egnacio's watch," said Pedro, "so we do know she was there. We can surmise that Egnacio was already dead as hers were on top of his prints, not under. Camilla could not have expected Marianne, Herbert, then you, Sally, to interfere with her plan." Smiling at her, and apparently addressing her, he went on.

"What Camilla and Roberto should have done, at this point was run with the diamonds they had, but as they were suddenly 'available' on the dress, Roberto wanted the last eleven diamonds. We know that it was not Roberto running across the square from your apartment, he was on duty elsewhere. It was Greg and whatever he's up to is not connected with these murders, although it was an unexpected bonus for the killers as it gave them breathing space."

After checking his notes briefly, Pedro continued with the official theory about the attack on Pamela who had heard her assailant wheezing.

"Several witnesses have confirmed José's account of a breathless woman in her sixties struggling past the café, under your apartment balcony Pamela, so it looks as if Camilla was your attacker. We think she was after your flat keys and, because you were gripping your bag so tightly, she assumed they would be in it. As it turned out though, the keys were still in your hand and didn't fall until you were in the ambulance."

Pedro paused to take an even longer sip of wine, wondering how they were taking his reconstruction of events. Of course, they would never know, for sure, what Camilla and Roberto and the others had thought because, apart from Herbert, everyone was dead. But this was not a presentation for the courts and a little speculation made it all easier to explain and fit the pieces together so that they made sense.

Chapter 37 – The Story Continues

"So, who killed Marianne and the Frau?" asked Sally, impatient to get to the end.

"Ok," Pedro resumed, "When Herbert found Marianne in the skip, there was a lot of blood, but the forensic team also found ricin in her system. Ricin was Camilla's killing method of choice. Marianne had been questioning why the profits from the Frau's thefts were so low this year and was highly suspicious about both Egnacio's death and that Camilla had sent her into the jeweller's shop alone. We think that Camilla went to the Mediterraneo and had a meal with her, to talk through their 'issues'. She used this as an opportunity to 'salt' Marianne's food with the same ricin that she later used to lace the chocolate sent to Frau Schmeckler."

They all nodded, clearly horrified at how casually Camilla had disposed of the obstacles in her way.

"They also found her fingerprints in the office used by Marianne, The owner had never met Camilla except, briefly, at that one meal, so she must have gone back, after the café closed, to take away the accounts that Marianne held for their 'cooperative', expecting her to be dead by then, but, as with the Frau later, she badly miscalculated the speed that ricin kills when eaten as opposed to injected."

Sally shuddered.

It was such a horrible image.

Pedro refilled her glass and continued. "We think Marianne was still alive, but groggy, when her murderer returned. Camilla must have walked her outside and pushed her into the skip. She already had plans to put the blame for everything on Roberto, who was not really her son by the way, so, thinking on her feet about the way he'd killed the jeweller, she probably went back into the restaurant kitchen, grabbed a chef's knife, finished Marianne off in the skip with it, then, after rinsing it, put it in plain sight with the cutlery in the dishwasher that had already gone through, ready to be unloaded in the morning – she just put the dishwasher through again."

Sitting on the arm of Sally's chair, he continued. "The police looked at all the knives in the kitchen and couldn't find blood traces on any, but the day after the restaurant was cleared to reopen, the chef insisted that he would not have put one of his favourite filleting knives in the 'heathen' machine and none of the staff would have dared touch his special set of German Henckels – the set and knife block had cost him well over two hundred euros!"

Next Pedro told them what he and Sofía had worked out. Once Marianne was out of the way, Camilla lost no time in sending the Frau a box of ricin-poisoned chocolate. It transpired that, as the Frau was, to put it politely, a 'bigger' woman than Marianne, she might recover enough to tell her story. Roberto, catching up on the crimes committed by the woman he thought was his mother, felt obliged to try and protect her. He knew the Frau was under guard and felt he had no option but to finish what Camilla had started, by smothering the Frau in the hospital.

Pedro continued the narrative. "Messing with the Port's street cameras was the least of the interference that Roberto ran for Camilla. He purloined Pamela's keys, handed in just as his shift ended, and swapped the dresses to retrieve the diamonds, without, hopefully, arousing suspicion."

"He couldn't have looked at Pamela's painting then," chirped Raoul, who, like Carlos, was utterly gripped by the story. "So, what happened at the end, in the fake Karkoff studio? You and your sergeant have been very secretive about it all week!"

Pedro grinned apologetically at his old friend, "Well, we needed to be. First, we had to make absolutely sure that there wasn't anyone else involved. The appearance of Sally's ex-boyfriend, Greg, for instance, was inopportune. Then we needed to examine all the emails and letters between Camilla and Roberto, to decide what their relationship was and see what their plans were – not least where the diamonds had gone." They all nodded understanding the difficulties.

"Camilla had sewn the diamonds onto her holiday clothing. She used plastic mounts, so they wouldn't trigger a Custom's scanner alert – they would all just look like gaudy holiday garments. The two suitcases had only contained Camilla's clothes. There was only one airline ticket and that was in her name."

He paused for a sip of water before continuing.

"We can only speculate what happened at the end. We know that Camilla used ricin again, on Roberto, who, believing she really was his mother, probably had no idea that he was at risk. We know that they had quarrelled several times over the last few days, but, deep down, he must still have trusted her. From the forensics evidence we know that he started to go dizzy whilst 'in the bathroom', hence the urine spillage on the floor. At that point he knew!"

There was a knock at the door and everyone in the room, apart from Pedro, jumped.

It was only a waiter coming in to take orders.

Pedro waited until the boy returned with fresh drinks, before continuing. His audience was impatient to hear more, so it was fortunate that orders were simple and the waiter was quick.

"Staggering into the kitchen, it appears that he confronted her. There were signs of a struggle and evidence that, at some point, he had his hands round her neck trying to strangle her. Unluckily for Camilla, she had just started washing away the evidence of their last meal together when he attacked her. He flung her away from him, so she lost her balance, then he grabbed a dirty dinner knife and thrust it into her neck. Even if she had survived the beating, the attempted strangulation and the stabbing, the knife he grabbed was his, from the meal, so there was enough ricin powder, still stuck to its surface to have finished her off, anyway!"

"Why?" asked Sally, "She used ricin twice and failed to kill her victims both times, so why would it have worked this time?"

Pedro replied. "Ahh, finally, she must have learned from her mistakes and used every last speck of the ricin that she had in stock, mixing it all with Roberto's meal. He had a penchant for sauces with steak, so for his last supper, she had cooked Steak

Bearnaise, lacing the bearnaise sauce with eight times the amount of powder she'd used in the Frau's chocolates. Roberto had a lot of problems, he was short-tempered, violent and a bully, but he had nothing on Camilla Perez. I cannot condone murder, but the court system has been saved a huge expense trying to prove all the details I've given you tonight. Your discretion is appreciated, you may repeat only what is necessary to the few who need to know, but you have all had some involvement in this case from the start, so we felt it only fair to tell you" They all nodded, understanding his position.

"But," he continued, "be wary. Lola and José don't really need to know the whole sordid tale – it would be unkind. Just tell Lola enough to make sure that she understands that she had a narrow escape from a burgeoning psychopath and José that his evidence about the woman probably broke the case."

He raised his glass to Raoul and Carlos, "I am sorry this account has eaten into your special evening, but I know that you would have gone away worrying about Pamela and Sally's safety, without knowing, for sure, that the investigation is over and the murderers are dead. Now, everyone, except Sally, please go back to the party. Raoul and Carlos have still a few hours before they need to leave on their honeymoon."

The small group slipped back into the noisy reception area.

They were lucky. The guests were enjoying themselves so much that not even the grooms had been missed.

Raoul's promises to keep the party small, in keeping with the small ceremony that had preceded it, had been thwarted by his inherent fear that one of his many friends might be offended by exclusion. *Friends!* Carlos thought, *more like passers-by, slight acquaintances and every single customer that the Raoul's family vineyard and bodega have ever had! It is just as well nearly everyone drinks wine and Raoul's family have been more than generous about providing it!*

"Now you know why it was a good idea to marry me," teased Raoul in his ear, picking up Carlos's thoughts intuitively, as only someone truly in love can. They silently toasted each other and started to circulate the room.

Pamela was surprised, but pleased, to see the Garcia family sitting at a small table, chatting to the mayor. It was just as well that Señor Garcia was proven to be an innocent bystander and cleared of being complicit in the smuggling, else she would have lost her commission.

As she approached, the mayor was hijacked by a laughing young couple, who were obviously keen to check his calendar for their own wedding.

Señor Garcia ushered her to the mayor's vacated seat. "We are so glad to see you, we have a huge favour to ask, please. Pedro has said that the main dress, the one you actually painted, is ruined!"

His wife interrupted, "I cannot believe all those diamonds were on our baby's dress – everyone is talking about it!"

"Yes dear, I know, you've reminded me several times! But you just don't expect a dress that cost as much as that one, expensive though it was, to have ten times its value in diamonds sewn onto it! Anyway Pamela," he turned back towards her, "the murders and the dress and the part my daughter's portrait played in unravelling the crime have become something of a talking point, so may we ask, when you are well enough to continue the portrait can you please leave the dress details as they are, with all the diamonds on it?"

Pamela wasn't at all surprised. She had already decided that the notoriety of the portrait and the story behind the dress would add value to the painting if left it as it was! The other dress was the same material. The reflections of light on skin and the details on seam edges would be close enough to the original for the young sitter to wear it so she could finish the face, flesh and hair details, and complete the portrait.

"Of course, Señor," she replied, "Senorita Garcia can wear the dress in my studio for the last few sittings, the police don't need it." The conversation then drifted to arranging times for the portrait to be continued.

Once they were alone, Pedro refilled Sally's glass and told her about Sofía's offer. Sally was delighted for him; she understood straight away, that this was a huge opportunity for him. Sleuthing was clearly something he was good at. It would be far more interesting for him than walking a beat, however pleasant it might be in the port.

Most of all, though, she was delighted that he thought it appropriate to talk it over with her. It had felt natural to him to include her in his decision-making process. After they had talked about the job and agreed he should jump at the opportunity it presented, they wandered back to the wedding reception.

They leaned, naturally into each other as they weaved among the guests, greeting friends and enjoying the buzz.

Always Right

Chapter 38 – Another Sunday

It was now two weeks since the excitement across the bay.

Greg had followed the story with interest, scanning the local, free English papers for information about what had happened. The police had been quite thorough about interviewing everyone they could find. To his annoyance, they had even interviewed *him* about his appearance in the square, shortly after the attack on Pamela.

He stuck to his story that he'd come to Spain to try and get back together with Sally but had lacked the courage to approach her.

He'd glossed over the notion that he had been running away and said he'd dashed to his bike because he'd been embarrassed and wanted to leave quickly, before Sally returned to the flat.

He told them that he'd got as far as the apartment door and seen the note from Pamela, so had realised that Sally could not be at home.

At that point, he claimed, he decided that the whole idea was stupid. He had run back to his bike and gone for a drive along the coast to clear his head. The police had accepted his story.

They really were quite dim.

Was it likely that he would really want that bitch back?

Still, this was not a good time to carry out his revenge. He'd expected this visit to be only a reconnaissance trip, his visit to the flat was mainly to check its security. If it had been easy to get in, he would have pushed forward with his plan, but it wasn't, it was a decent lock.

He had run because he'd heard a commotion on a lower floor.

Greg was surprised to see a photo of Sally in the paper he had just picked up from reception. Today she was in it because last Saturday she was at some weird wedding ceremony. Shocked, he paused to doublecheck the information. No, she had not been the bride, she was a bridesmaid! Last week, she'd been in it because there was a splutter about the week of murders, naming her as the person who found the first victim. The story had finished after a brief statement from the police saying that the case was closed as the murderers had killed themselves!

Really, the police were dimmer than dim!

He'd seen the wheezing woman in the square on the day of the attack on Pamela, when he ran past her.

She smelled.

She had a sour, sweaty smell that only people with sensitive noses like his would notice, but he knew she had sweated her way up the steps to Sally's apartment because he could smell the lingering stench of her, as he ran out.

It wasn't rocket science to grasp that she must have had something to do with the attack on Pamela!

A few days later, he'd smelled her again, in the port.

Turning to see where she was, he saw her unlocking a door near the kitchen door of a beach café, provocatively called 'Lola'.

On the opposite side of the street, he'd noticed some of the entrance doors were recessed, giving him several possible vantage points from which to watch what was happening up and down the street. So good were they that, outside one, he had also found an old wooden kitchen chair, where the occupant would sometimes sit to chat with passing neighbours. Even better, it looked as if the occupant must be away because his mailbox was full of advertising flyers.

Glossy leaflets for rugs and carpets, Really?

Settling himself in, he spent a few days watching the comings and goings at the flat. It was clear that the policeman was up to no good and the woman was up to her ears in whatever was going on.

Frankly, he decided, he was bored with them both.

They were a distraction he didn't need.

They were also drawing too much attention to Sally and he didn't want her in the limelight. With police hovering round her all the time, his task would be even more difficult.

Luckily the lock on the smelly woman's flat door was old and easy to manipulate. Even he had no problem opening it, despite his minimal lock-picking skills, garnered from the internet on his phone when he'd explored ways to get into Sally's locked apartment.

He'd even been able to adapt some cheap tools he'd picked up from a Chinese bargain shop, nearby.

It didn't take him long to find the diamonds, lined

up neatly, ready for whatever Camilla was going to do with them.

He decided to leave them there, for now, he could pick them up when he got back. It was a fair bet that nobody besides Camilla and Roberto had any idea how many diamonds she had.

Right now, however, it was important that they did not suspect they'd had a visitor.

It was hot in the rubber gloves, but he wanted to leave no trace for the police, later.

She would be back soon and he needed to intervene and end whatever they were up to once and for all.

He'd read up on the murders carefully, as each was reported in the press, so he knew about ricin having been used. A quick internet search showed him what it looked like in powder form.

Sure enough, hidden at the back of the bathroom cabinet he found a plastic bag with a substantial amount of white powder.

Now, where to put it?

There was a shop-bought cardboard packet of some kind of sauce on the kitchen counter and, in the fridge, was a plate with two raw steaks on it, 'breathing' – clearly tonight's meal.

He'd come prepared. Using a penknife, he had chosen for its fine blade, he unsealed the bottom of the sauce packet.

Making a small incision in the bottom of the bag, he found inside, he carefully spooned in all of the ricin.

Using double-sided sticky tape, he then resealed the inner bag by sticking it to the inside of the box, in turn sealing the box using more tape.

It was fool proof. It looked like a factory seal and hopefully, they would both eat their meal with sauce.

If not, he would only have one person to deal with when he came back for the diamonds.

Returning the packet, where he found it, he let himself out of the apartment.

When he returned, early on Monday evening, he heard the woman wheezing and struggling in the kitchen. The man had clearly been the only one to eat his steak with sauce. Now he appeared to be strangling the woman, *He must think that she poisoned him, how deliciously ironic! She had obviously been trying to please him.*

Unobserved, he'd watched, feeling like he imagined a spider would, savouring its prey enmeshed in a web.

It had been quite thrilling.

A bit like a dress rehearsal for what he had planned for Sally, but that would not be this crude.

When the man finally collapsed and the woman broke free, Greg casually walked into the kitchen and brushed past her as he headed towards the sink. He had put the gloves back on, before he entered, so he had no problem picking up the bearnaise smeared knife and plunging it deeply into her neck.

Before he left the flat, he pushed the man's body a little, so that its weight blocked the kitchen's fire escape door.

Wandering past the bedroom, he decided to add a little mystery to the pot, for the fun of it – a little game with the police.

There were three packed suitcases in the larger bedroom, two clearly belonged to the woman, the third to the man.

He took the man's case to the smaller bedroom and carefully unpacked its contents into the sort of drawers they had probably been in.

Helping himself to the ticket, the various currencies in the man's wallet and the man's passport, in case he could use it in his own project, he threw them into the, now empty suitcase, ready to take with him.

On his way out, he pocketed the eleven diamonds still on the workroom table. He knew there were probably more, but he had been there long enough. Eventually the policeman would be missed – it was time to go.

Once the suitcase was empty again, he would abandon it in the airport tomorrow, on his way home to the UK. It would be another bit of fun to make up for this wasted trip. With luck, he would have a good view of the airport's security police worrying about what it might have inside and trying to find its owner.

With several thousand pounds in diamonds in his pocket, his trip to Spain had been extremely profitable so he would let the excitement die down, for now. Perhaps this chapter of his life was over? After all, he'd certainly been well compensated.

Maybe he would leave her alone.

Of course, if he ever did come out to Spain, again, he would be better organised.

At least, now, he knew where she was.

Find out more about Sally's life in Spain on her blog at www.orme.buzz